UP WITH THE CROWS

THE UNSYLUM SERIES BOOK ONE

ZOE PARKER

xoxo Zoe Parker

CONTENTS

This is to all of you.
Darkness rests in every soul, balancing out the whole. Give it wings
to fly away but it'll always return another day.

The Unsylum Series Book One

Up With The Crows

Zoe Parker

Birds have wings; they're free; they can fly where they want, when they want. They have the kind of mobility many people envy.
Roger Tory Peterson

CHAPTER ONE

Birds born in cages think that flying is an illness. ~*Alejandro Jodorowsky*

A DATE SHOULDN'T MAKE you sleepy in the first twenty minutes.

As he drones on, my jaw cracks from repeated yawning. I shake myself to try and wake up. When the heat vent above us kicks on, the air hits my hand and announces that while I semi-dozed, I drooled a little on my hand. Eyes steady on him, watching for any sign that he's not just a talkative robot, I use the linen tablecloth to clean my hand. Beggars can't be choosers, and I believe in taking advantage of the opportunities presented to me

Straightening, I'm determined to stay awake for the remainder of the date. Then again, he hasn't exactly noticed me napping while he's gone on and on about his entire life.

On our *first* date. I bet he's the type of guy that tracks his daily fiber intake, something about him screams that he gets constipated easily.

Honestly, mean thoughts aside, I should be paying attention to—possibly enthralled by—every word coming out of his mouth. Especially since this is the first real date I've had in a year—not counting my drunken escapades. Those weren't dates with anyone but the gyno. I'm careful but also paranoid, in this day and age we have to be. If I had unprotected sexy times, with the way my luck works, I'd get the supercharged UTI to end all UTIs and die alone with thirty cats and a pee bag strapped to my leg.

Not that cats are bad, I like cats. My allergies don't.

The entire point is, this is a real date—with food that you don't have to shell in a wicker bowl—and I should be more appreciative of it. Should.

Curious now, I eye Steven, and try to gauge exactly how much attention he's paying to me. From the way he keeps talking, with that practiced smile hovering on his face, I'd say not much. He's too busy listing his life accomplishments and how much everyone at his job appreciates him.

This date is an obvious mistake, I jumped at it—like the desperate woman I am—when he sent me a message on the 'KissingCupids' dating app. It was politely worded and contained all the ridiculous keywords that make women break out the lipstick, including me. Without being superficial, I should've known that a guy as attractive as him, asking me on a date without having a bit of conversation first, had something wrong with him. All the warning bells in my head should've gone off. Or they did, and I ignored them. I have major issues with impulse control, it's why I'm banned from the Home Shopping Network.

Focusing on his face and with genuine effort, I attempt to smile. It falls flat, despite my best efforts, and turns into a frown when the plastic smile on his face doesn't change one bit. There's not even a pause in his onslaught of fun facts about himself, and I know he saw me wipe my hand.

There's something fucked up with that.

To make matters worse, he takes a conversational leap into the subject of his requirements for a prospective wife. Morbidly fascinated I pay close attention to them, not because I'm interested but because I want to see if he surprises me with his answers.

Of course he doesn't.

A petite sized woman who maintains a clean, orderly household; who never drinks, only eat light foods—like lettuce. Works full time to ease the burden from her 'doting' husband, while also solo raising the children until they're old enough for him to 'make sense of'. She's then expected to cook three square meals a day, with dessert. Iron his clothes with crisp creases.

Gracefully, and yes—he used that word—hosts parties for his work cronies, while looking glamorous and happy, yes, he used the word glamorous too. His dream wife is apparently a maid/nanny/ hostess/full-time sugar mama, instead of a life partner equal to him in all things.

I think there's a chance that this guy was hugged a bit too much by mommy.

Don't get me wrong, there's nothing wrong with someone doing any of these things, if that makes them happy, but kids are a job unto themselves and a hard one. If the father is present, he should do as much as the mom.

The bar he's setting is unrealistically high and I'm not sure that it'll ever be met. I think in his case the unfortunate wife will do all the heavy lifting, while he's sipping a cocktail by the pool.

That doesn't sit right with me. I think I've stupidly gone on a date with a Stepford-husband.

Honestly though, would knowing this have stopped me from coming on this date? Nope, because I'm an average, lonely woman, in her late thirties who still hasn't found a long-term partner. I crave love like everyone else, the need for someone to come home to and cuddle with after a bad day. Hell, maybe even have kids with. The normal white picket fence shit. Luck, however, is not on my side. I've yet to have a relationship last beyond a few months and nothing I do salvages them.

I've gotten the line, 'It's not you, it's me' so many times I should make a shirt that says it to make it easier on them to get it over with.

God, I'm bitter as hell.

I could do worse than him, he's a good-looking guy; dressed rather nice, if a bit overdressed, in a light gray suit that was obviously tailored to fit him. It probably cost more than I've had in my bank account at any given time, in years. His wavy hair is honey colored, cut in a style that flatters his face while looking natural in the process. A vivid set of robin's egg blue eyes stand out starkly on his tanned face.

Even without the eyes, his face belongs on a coin somewhere in Roman history. High cheekbones and a strong prominent jaw shows that at least one of his parents has good genes. And I'm pretty sure there are dimples in both cheeks too. I'm surprised he's not a movie star or a model in a catalog, instead of a portfolio manager who looks for dates on an app.

Going purely on how he looks—in theory—he's perfect for me. Just looking at him would make most women get all gaga. He's over six-feet tall with the kind of smile that should get him plenty of company. His lips are full, and kind of plush for a man and his teeth are a bright, almost blinding white and incredibly straight. Definitely, a braces kid, but it was worth the result. On top of the physical attributes, he has a six-figure job, his own house, and drives a car that looks like he bought it yesterday.

The suit and the way he carries himself prove those bits of info he provided are potentially true. But... I feel absolutely nothing for the guy. Zero. Nada. My vagina is so dry that I'm surprised there isn't sand in my underwear.

It's disappointing to say the least.

He's a like long-winded preacher on a hot Sunday morning kind of dull. Why does it always happen this way? Is it the creepy factor? Considering it, I decide it's not and face the truth of my loserness. If he were in debt up to his eyeballs and considering selling his kidney to buy a bag of weed, I'd think he was the best guy ever.My dating radar is completely and utterly broken.

The last time I had a date that I relatively enjoyed, the guy showed up with his shoes on the wrong feet, wearing only one sock. I hadn't dated for months at the time, not even the occasional one nightery, so I ignored his 'rumpled' appearance, choosing instead to go with it. Idiotically, we started drinking. As the night progressed, and the alcohol flowed freely, he somehow lost his shirt and, man, those abs were hard to resist. Not that I did, at least I don't think I did. It's still a hazy memory.

In my defense, we ended up so drunk that the only reason I remember his face—okay, so those abs and his face, his name is lost in time somewhere—is because I took a picture on my phone. He is one of the reasons my Gyno knows me by sight. After having drunken sex, or the suspicion I did—with someone whose name I can't remember—the smartest choice I made in that entire situation was to take a trip to the doc. Thankfully, one of the condoms in my purse was gone, and all the tests came back clean.

It's a shame that the probably-had-it sex wasn't memorable, because then I'd have something more than a nagging worry about being that irresponsible. I'd know exactly how good or bad it was and having that clinging memory of something I shared with another person. I'll admit I still occasionally hook up—ha, not lately but thinking it makes me feel better—but I don't drink at the same time anymore. Alcohol and I combined always results in havoc. Always. Usually it's the kind that I regret the next day, but not every single time. I can't lie and say that every moment of my life has been that pitiful.

Although, the fact that I came on this date, while ignoring my common sense, might get itself filed in the pitiful pile.

"Will it be my place or your place after dinner?" he asks. I swear I hear that awful sound of a record needle scraping in my head as I focus on him. He has my complete attention now.

"I'm sorry, what?" I ask semi-hoping I heard him wrong.

"For sex," he says so nonchalantly that I think he had more emotion talking about his job than having sex with me. I'm not sure whether to laugh at him or hit him in the face with my plate.

"I didn't realize that was a guaranteed thing. Is there a hidden stipulation for that in the contract for the dating site that I met your ass on?" I ask, lifting my phone to pull up the app. I'm not actually going to read the terms of service, but I am going to read our conversation and make sure I didn't miss agreeing to have sex with him on the first date. Sure, I've done it, but that's not the point. There was no expectation of it and him having one annoys the ever-living shit out of me.

"I assumed, my mistake." He finally loses that creepy smile off his face. "If you'll excuse me, I need to use the restroom." Frowning at him, but seeing no reason to argue with him going to the bathroom, I wave him away.

After twenty-minutes, with no sign of him returning, I

have no choice but to accept that he isn't coming back. I suspected it after the first five but I'm nothing if not stubborn. I was determined to give him a chance to be a decent human being and pay his half of the bill. This type of guy is one of the many reasons I have an incredibly small amount of faith in romance. Grabbing the check, I look dejectedly at the minuscule amount of money in my wallet and head up to the cashier.

Not having as much cash as I thought, I end up digging through the bottom of my purse, where things get lost, for change.

"Here ya go," I sit the sticky items in my hand on the counter, "You get a free half-piece of gum and some lint." Both are stuck to the dirty quarter that finishes the last bit of the change I have. My eyes burn, but I push my way through it. Steven doesn't care that I won't have food this week because he ditched. I attempt to smile at the cashier who looks at me with a mix of pity and disgust, yeah, that's not an uncommon look.

"Do you want a receipt?"

"Yea, please."

As I wait for him to give me the receipt, I get lost in my thoughts. Considering that he bailed on a thirty-dollar dinner, it's possible that Steven's wealth is all a façade. That explains why he ordered double portions, something someone in his kind of shape wouldn't normally do. I have to wonder if he planned on making me pay the bill even if we had planned on sleeping together.

Now that I analyze some of his—what I thought was eccentric—behavior, all the signs were there. The way he turned his 'Rolex' away when I asked to see it, not that I'd know if it were fake. I've never seen a real one. Or how he had an almost perfect life, that was probably fake too. Hell, maybe that's how he affords all those expensive props because some dumbass like me pays all the bills. A new horror fills my mind. Oh, shit what if he's married?

That Ken-doll mother—

"Ma'am, can you please continue your tirade outside? You're disturbing the other customers." The nasally voice of the cashier breaks into my mental tangent.

Turning my attention to the pimply-faced boy, I open my mouth to apologize but the smug look on his face changes my mind. "It's Denny's dude, it's not exactly a hundred-dollar plate place. There's a homeless guy in the corner with pee stains on his pants." He opens his mouth to argue and then he looks at the homeless guy, who's actually in the corner with pee stains on his pants and shuts his mouth.

Without another word, I grab my receipt and my money-less purse and drag my ass out to my car.

STOPPING outside of the ancient contraption that—out of pride—I still call a car, I peel the corner of the plastic grocery bag off the window. Sliding my arm through the hole, I pop the lock and open the door. Yes, there's no window, and I still lock the doors, but for me, it's a point of principle. Fixing the bag, I climb inside and pull the door shut only to look over and find that the passenger window is in pieces on the seat. The desire to cry again hits me hard, with a tight throat I fight it back with a sharp bite to my inner cheek. On the seat, on top of the shards of safety glass, is a note written on a copy of my resume.

Sorry for breaking your window, I didn't realize there was a bag on the other side. I didn't steal anything because I felt bad about breaking it. God bless.

Why the hell did they end their note with God bless? I mean come on! They broke into my car, you can't bless someone you tried to steal from. That's gotta be blasphemy of some kind, or a one-way ticket to a special kind of hell when they die. Angrily, I swipe at the tears streaking down my face, I hate being an emotional crier. If I'm sad I cry, if I'm happy I cry, if I'm mad I cry. It sucked as a kid and sucks even more as an adult.

Sniffling, I turn the car on and wait, the customary two minutes with my ears covered, for the fan belt to stop its awful caterwauling. I pat the dashboard affectionately, Herbette and I have gone through some shit together. I've had this car since the day I got my license. Mom parked it in the driveway with a big polka-dot bow on it. Of course, back then it was in great shape, brand new and shiny. I'm pretty sure it only had forty miles on it when I started it up the first time.

Getting it was one of the happiest days of my life; we spent the evening driving around with the windows down while singing loudly to eighties music. This car has been where I cried the most, where I lost my virginity, and where I got my first speeding ticket. So many memories inside of this wonderful, rusted metal member of my family. Now she's twenty-three years old and, if I could, I'd retire her.

The whole too-poor-to-buy-a-new-one thing interferes with that.

Turning the radio on, I make a face, but would rather have the background noise. The soothing classical music that I listened to—one time—twenty-two years ago, is now all that plays in the car. Somehow, in one of my drunken teenage moments, I got gum in the hole for the knob. The knob that's been missing since that day. Of course, that was back when I had friends before they left me behind to pursue their dreams of farming. Together. Without me.

Come on Mel, you sound a bit twatty don't you?

Sniffling again, I wipe my snotty nose with a tissue from

the emergency pack I keep in the console. I only had two friends in high school, Jason and Charmaine. Back then it was the three of us conquering the world. We did everything together and having that closeness with them made the crapshoot of high school bearable. That dream of going to the same college and being best friends forever, all came crashing down on me the day after graduation. Jason proposed to Charmaine who then decided that they couldn't be my friends anymore. To her, I was a distraction for Jason from the life goals she had planned for them, you know, their sudden dreams of farming.

Talk about a complete one-eighty.

Jason looked like an eager puppy as he grabbed her hand went off to change the world of produce and become famous entrepreneurs. Now he weighs four hundred pounds, has no hair, and sports a bad case of adult acne. She's lumpy like a cheap pillow and smokes two packs of cigarettes a day. I know for a fact that she also cheats on him religiously with the truckers at the Que-Mart. The goal they had of starting an organic farm and living the green life crumbled on their heads because they have six kids, ten dogs and live in a trailer outside of town. No farm, no green life. Just a yard full of old appliances and broken-down cars that weave around the store-bought swimming pool that she washes laundry in. Both work at Greg's Grocery, not that it's shameful to work there, but it's not the organic farm they dumped me for.

Honestly, I've never seen two people hate each other as much as they do now.

There's a teeny tiny part of me that wants to celebrate their misfortune, the rest of me kicks its ass. Never, ever, should a person feel happy about someone's misery. There's something abjectly wrong with that. I *can* be happy that I wasn't dumb enough to be the one to date Jason. Instead, I went off to college to get my useless bachelor's in human resources, that's only use thus far is a fancy, framed walnut-cracking tray.

Still, in all that misery and bitterness, at least they both have jobs. I seem to run into constant issues keeping one. Bad luck follows me around like a stalker, always getting into my life and messing everything up. My most recent job, working as a dog groomer, was great. I love dogs, and for some reason, they love me back, never had one give me issue. It's their owners that I ran into problems with. Dyeing your dog's fur is yuck, the colored spray that washes off is fine, but the actual dye is horrible for their skin and their digestion. Dogs lick themselves.

All I tried to do was explain to her—what my boss *told* me to explain to her—about the dangers of dyeing your dog's fur. She clobbered me with her purse and demanded I be fired, or she was suing the business. Considering that it's a small-town business, with a single owner and me—the only other employee—Sandy, my boss, didn't have a choice. She canned me with a week's severance pay.

Which I used the last of to buy that dickhead's dinner.

I have every right in the world to feel like shit right now. However temporary it needs to be. I can't dwell on it, but I can take my minute to sulk. My small hidden window of time to let the hurt from the entire fiasco out a little.

Finally, the fan belt decides to cooperate and stop phoning home to its alien kin; I suck up the sad crap and leave. The drive home is uneventful and takes me around fifteen minutes. The drive's view consists of mostly corn-fields and trees. Driving super slow past my house I go to the end of the street and turn around. With a little bit of reverse, forward, reverse—ohgodIalmosthittheneighborscar, I was able to back the car into the only parking spot left on the block. At least this far from the house I can mostly avoid my mother. I know that makes me a complete jerk, but she has somewhere around fifteen cats. Fifteen! I have a severe allergy to all of them.

Plus, the whole hoarding thing.

I love my mom, she's great, she's just a bit of a keep everything person. Okay, not everything but she has every cat themed comic book, toy, and piece of Tupperware in existence. I'm not kidding, not one bit. There's a narrow path that winds from room to room with every inch of the walls of *stuff* covered in cat hair. Lots and lots of cat hair. So much hair that, if I walk by when she has a window open, I break out in hives. I've tried a therapist, an interventionist, throwing stuff out... you name it, to help her. I realized at some point I only made it worse, I can't make her take care of herself, she has to be willing.

Hoarding is a serious mental illness that many people don't realize is an actual illness. Having this issue doesn't make her a bad person. Mom still goes to church every Sunday, every Wednesday and to every single optional service they have. She pays her taxes, even mows her grass— shocker—the yard itself is pristine. She's kind and giving, I couldn't have asked for a better mom, but the cats and the things all over is too much. Living in that house was killing me. The doctor literally said my lungs were getting damaged.

I moved into the small one-room building in the backyard. We framed out the inside and put in a little shower, toilet and kitchen area—I even have a rug. The shed is 12x12 with enough space for me to basically exist, but do little else. I'm perfectly fine with it. Mom wanted me to stay close without me having to get Catfur's Lung living in her house. The whole rent-free thing helps too. Truth be told, I'm pretty sure that it's the only reason I'm not some homeless bum living in the park, surviving on the pigeon seed people throw out.

Taking a deep breath to prepare myself, I get out of the

car and hoof it up the street, cutting through the half yard we share with our neighbor to bypass the front, where my Mom looks out the picture window like a... cat. Wow, it's weird and yet accurate to think that. My Mom is that nosey neighbor who knows if you've come home late and did the walk of shame. She also likes watching the cars go by sometimes, with a sweet, distracted smile on her face. So, cat definitely fits her.

As soon as I get close to my humble abode, the boys start making a racket that I can hear over the lawn mower, which needs to retire more than my car. Pausing, I look at our neighbor—he's a bit of a peculiar one. He watches my Mom when she's outside puttering around the yard, but not in that call-the-police way, but more in the I-wanna-touch-your-butt way.

Ew, now that I think about it.

His name is Earl, and he's got a comb-over that he's determined to keep no matter how many times I make a comment about it. He's had it for so long that he has tan lines from it. It shows that he's a dedicated type person. Staring at him on his ancient mower, trying to watch our house and not get caught doing it is a bit amusing. His hair used to be bright orange, but as he's aged, it's silvered out quite a bit, and he still dresses in clothes from the 70s, but some people consider that back in style. He's a bit plump in the middle, but his legs are so skinny and white that they look like popsicle sticks when he wears shorts.

As he meets my eyes, I smile and wave at him. I can see why mom secretly stares back at him. He has a pretty pair of green eyes that remind me of the tall grass that grows outside of town, in the spring. Vivid and bright and always with a sparkle in them. I give him a lot of shit, but when it comes down to it, he's sweet as hell. After his cheeks pinken to a ruddy red, he waves back and turns his riding lawn mower in the opposite direction.

Making him blush is the highlight of my day sometimes.

With a furtive glance at the quiet house, I run a little to get to the shed. "Guys shut up before she hears you!" I whisper fiercely, while trying to enter the combination to the lock on the door. The noise increases instead of decreases and I know it's because I spoil them rotten. The only men I manage to keep in my life are obnoxious feather brains. Finally, my stiff fingers work, I pop the lock off and duck inside.

"Rub dem titties all over me, baby!" Loki, the alpha male of the flock, yells from the kitchen counter where he's pecking at the door of his cage.

With a sigh, I turn to him and say, "Loki, I have to teach you more words than that." I admit that I say this every single time I enter the house and the parrot yells that particular phrase—which I think is his favorite—or some of the other colorful ones. Like, 'just spit on it' or 'it's so big' for example. Loki, my adorable African Gray Parrot, is a rescue bird and his former owner was a porn producer. I'd bet my left kidney this bird knows more about sexual positions than I ever will. He's also a big softie despite having the vocabulary of a hooker.

When I unlatch the cage door, to prove my point, he follows the path of the rope strung all over the ceiling to the rafter above me and hops down to my shoulder to nuzzle my cheek. A loud tapping sound pulls my gaze back to the second cage on the kitchen counter where Hardy, God bless his blind ass, is pecking away at an old ashtray that's leaning against the wall outside of his cage. A left over from when I used to smoke. I'd love to say I quit, instead I've gotten more sophisticated. I vape now. I even make my own vape juice which is incredibly cheaper than buying it.

Not that I currently have any.

Hardy is a blind parakeet, another rescue bird that was left when his former owner died. No one wanted him, so I took him. He's adorable and loves to make little whistle noises and since he can't see he mistakes everything for bird seed. Everything. Crossing the small room, I lightly bump his leg with my finger to let him know to climb on. With an excited squawk, he climbs on and does his happy dance where he bounces up and down with his feathers fluffed out.

I use my thumb to kind of hold him in place, as he gets excited and takes a tumble sometimes.

"Dick." Willis, the last of my trio of men, calls from his hiding spot next to the patched-up inflatable mattress that makes up the bulk of my bedroom furniture. As in all of it. Willis is a cockatiel and is named after a man who is somewhat famous and as bald as he is. Completely and utterly bald, the crazy bird plucks out his own feathers and then insults you when you look at him.

A year ago, when I went to the city for a job interview, that I bombed horribly, I found a couple of homeless guys discussing how to eat him. For ten bucks they gave him to me. I'll freely admit that he's a bit deranged, I think all three of them are, but most of it is from trauma inflicted upon them. People aren't the only ones affected by such things.

We at least have the chance to get it treated and understood.

Crossing to his cage, I open the door and attempt to rub the top of his bald little head, but he nips my finger. Ungrateful butthole. Giving him a dirty look, I turn to dig through my small plastic wardrobe and get my pajamas out. Putting Loki on the rope, I climb into the only remotely luxurious part of this house—the shower. I found it at a church sale, still in the shrink wrap—I even installed it myself. Relatively without issue—mostly—after a *tiny* flood in the backyard and a few leaks here and there.

Done with a quick shower, I look through my small, empty pantry while brushing my teeth. I'm not hungry but I've only had one meal, and I will be hungry later. There's nothing in there, no potted meat or even any unlabeled cans of mystery food. Opening the drawer at the bottom ends in another failure. All that's in there is bird food, which means the boys won't go hungry.

Going back to the sink to rinse my mouth out, I inwardly vent as I gargle.

Why do I have this shitty luck? Did I piss off some mystical so-and-so and get jinxed for the rest of my life? The dating scene isn't the only facet of my life that's going to hell. Finding a job is at the bottom of the pot with all the shit piled on it. In every single interview, something goes wrong. If I luck out and get the job, within two months, I get terminated for some off the wall reason. It's never legit ones like me being late or missing work, nope—it's always something weird.

Like the dog grooming job.

Or when I tried working at the Que-Mart, I was fired because the freezer shorted out in the middle of summer and all the cold stuff went bad. Somehow, that was my fault and my head rolled. Then you have my brief stint as an actual HR person, that lasted three entire days. I was fired for marking 'other' as my ethnicity on my application. They said it was a form of dishonesty.

How the hell do you fire someone for that?

The worst one to date, in my opinion, was the nursing home. I was briefly employed there as a CNA, briefly being a whole two hours. I was fired because I refused to stick my hand up this incredibly sweet lady's hoo-ha to pull her false teeth out of it. She liked to shove things up there, and I wasn't qualified to remove things from there. For refusing, I was fired on the spot by the head nurse, who should've been the one helping the old gal remove her burden. Isn't that part of the *nurse's* job?

The entire fiasco of my working career is a never-ending, depressing, clusterfuck. Considering how it's all worked out, how can I not feel a little sorry for myself for a second time today? Most people would. It doesn't matter that I'm annoying myself with the bitterness of my self-pity. I think it's deserved, today has just been the cherry on top of an entire lifetime of crap—

"Deeper baby, deeper," Loki says. A surprised laugh lifts me out of my dark mood. I give him a bit of side-eye because I swear that bird knew I needed to be poked at. I rub his feathered chest and tuck him and the other boys into their cages. It's bedtime for the lot of us, my brain needs to check out for a few hours, and I can't trust the three of them loose. Wearily, I climb onto my bed. It's not too late, but I'm emotionally wrung out.

The tip-tap of rain hitting the roof makes me groan, I forgot to put a bag over the passenger window. Flopping back onto the bed I decide to give up on life for a little while and nap.

CHAPTER TWO

Birds are a miracle because they prove to us there is a finer, simpler state of being which we may strive to attain.
~Douglas Coupland

WAKING UP SLOWLY, with my body sunk into the bed at an awkward angle, I roll over and hit the power switch for the built-in pump on the mattress. The roar of the small motor fills the former quiet of the room with a head pounding noise, as it slowly lifts my body. A necessary evil if you sleep on one of these as much as I do. They stretch and deflate in a constant vicious cycle, and this one has a new leak that I haven't found yet. I woke up with my ass resting on the floor and my feet in the air, a definite sign of a slow leak.

However, leaks or not, it's much better than sleeping on the concrete floor. I know this because I slept on that cold, hard floor for a few weeks before I could buy this mattress. It sucked. I don't want to do it again.

Speaking of doing it again, it's time to look at the help wanted ads. I may have horrible luck with jobs, but I still need to have one. Opening my outdated but functional tablet, I start searching for openings on all jobs on the city job board. When I find a few open interviews, I write them down. Those sometimes pan out for me because I don't have time to freak myself out beforehand. Beggars can't be choosers either and I'm definitely a beggar. Using the process I've honed from too many years of doing it, I weed out the legitimate jobs from the fakes. While making a list on a notepad and doing my best to ignore the rumbling of my stomach, I move through the lists and ads quickly. I've ignored an empty stomach for years too. Mom had a habit of forgetting to buy food and I had a habit of not saying anything.

She struggled financially, and I didn't want to be a burden. When I came home from college and couldn't keep a steady job, no matter how hard I tried, I had to figure out something. Moving out here to the shed doesn't change the fact that I'm still living with her, but it gives me some form of independence. The majority of people my age have successful careers and their own homes. Not me though, I can't hold a job long enough to even discover what having a career is all about.

God, Mel stop lamenting how bad your life is. You're alive, aren't you?

Oh, shut up common sense, no one was talking to you.

After marking as many of the jobs as I could find that I might be able to do, and filling out the applications I could online, I decide to clean up my room a bit. The birds are pretty good at going to the bathroom in their cages, but feathers and birdseed get everywhere. Digging out the vacuum I found on the curb for free, I use it to clean up the birdseed and I pick up the feathers.

Carefully, I sort through them keeping a few that I like for my collection. Yes, I collect feathers instead of shoes or knick knacks like normal people. Apparently, this started when I was a pint-sized two or three-year-old. Mom said I picked up a peacock feather one day at the zoo, and that started my mini-obsession with them. They're like gold to me. I have no idea why I like them so much, I just do.

Opening the other cabinet in the room, which is the only glass object in my house, I carefully add the feathers I picked from the boys' leavings to the gold metallic box that I designated specifically for them. The rest of the three shelves are occupied by feathers from a multitude of bird species. I tend to favor the ones that have hidden colors, like certain ducks or crows and ravens. Raven feathers tend to look purple and blue in the light, while crow feathers are a purple and green color. I don't have a feather from either species, but not for lack of trying. The birds are all over the place and yet, no matter how much I look, no dropped feathers. Swiping at non-existent dust, I make sure everything is in its place before I shut the door. Other than my boys these feathers are the most valuable thing I own. Purely sentimental, but they mean more than money to me.

As that ugly, twisted little Stoor would say, "My precious."

Smirking at my own silly thoughts, I finish cleaning up and find myself standing, once again, in front of the small, empty fridge. There's not even ketchup in there, this is bad. I lightly slam the door in frustration. My eyes go automatically to the change jar I keep on the fridge. Empty like everything else. I can go without food for tonight, but come tomorrow I'll start feeling ill. Grabbing a glass, I fill it up with water, chug it, and then repeat. The hunger pangs temporarily abate, but they'll return. They always do.

I'll have to brave my mom's house. She won't mind me taking a couple slices of bread and a piece of cheese. I can't go to an open interview with my stomach growling the whole time; people are super judgmental about those kinds of things, and I need a job. Quickly I check on the boys and then settle down with the tablet on the bean bag I found in the neighbor's garbage. Well, it was beside their garbage, but I asked before I took it. They were moving anyhow. I've washed it with the hose and Lysol, but it still smells faintly of pickles. I have no idea why, but it is what it is, and I can over-look that smell most of the time. Most of my furniture was found on a curb or in a dumpster.

Logging into KissingCupids I find my inbox empty. Not that I'm terribly surprised, especially after Steven, who is presumably the cream of the crop for this website. With a bit of an evil smile on my face I go to his profile and enter my rating of our date.

Two Stars: Steven has a nice watch, a nice suit and an empty wallet. He got the red light for the booty and the only stiff thing I got was the check he bailed on.

Honestly, I only gave him two stars because he was a good-looking guy and even though it's not significant in any part of my life, this website supposedly takes these reviews seriously. In fact, by their TOS, he should be suspended for stiffing me for the meal. My smile grows bigger as I type out an email to the admins of the site. Listing the time and date, the restaurant, the amount of the bill and how I paid it, I send screenshots of our conversation and agreement to meet.

Guys like him though, won't be stopped by my comments on a dating app.

Grabbing my beat-up notepad, I check over the list and feel a little hopeful because there are over a dozen jobs here. While I'm uptown at the open interviews, I'll also look for hiring signs in windows. Someone has to hire me; I'm a good worker and I need the money. Finishing up I stand with resolve. Time to brave the cat hell.

Just outside the door, in a beat-up plastic tub, I keep a pair of shoes and a sort-of suit of armor specifically for Mom's house. This way my normal stuff doesn't get cat hair on them. I look down at the yellowed unicorn slippers. Once upon a time they were glittery and white, not yellow with something green growing on them. One of them is also missing the horn. Grabbing the poncho out of the tub and a shower cap, I don my armor and, with a deep breath for bravery, head towards the back door. I don't need a key, because she never locks the damn thing. The light in the dining room is on which means she's napping in a chair in the living room.

I squash the guilt for dreading a trip into my childhood home, I genuinely love her but if she sees me, she's going to want to help me. I can't have that. Mom has enough of her own worries, her health, her collections… those cats. Quietly, I open the door and immediately push a furry almost-escapee back into the kitchen. Forcing myself to avoid looking anywhere but the small path that's in front of me, I creep towards the fridges. She has two of them and she keeps all her food in there, except canned food. The cats get into it if she doesn't.

The smell is awful, seriously awful. Cat urine and crap galore. I have no idea how she deals with it, I couldn't when I came back home from college. In the four years I was gone she quadrupled everything, including the cats. I couldn't even find my bed the night I returned and ended up sleeping in my car; it was the only way I could breathe. The next day I rolled up my sleeves to dig my bed out. Between covering everything in plastic sheets, and locking the cats out of my room—which Mom didn't like, but understood—I was able to make my room at least bearable while I stayed there; but I really wished she'd let me help her. These conditions aren't healthy.

I change the direction of my thoughts so guilt won't lodge itself in my brain and keep me in a shitty mood the rest of the night, I open the fridge, and dig out the bread and cheese to make a sandwich with. Once I'm done, I put them back exactly where I got them from. She notices when things are moved—I have no idea how. Tucking my treasures into a sandwich bag—also in the fridge—I turn and weave my way through the room full of cats to the back door. Turning, I slowly pull the door open and then ease it shut behind me, while carefully keeping an eye out for any runners.

The last time one of Mom's cats got out it was hit by a car. She cried for three days straight. No way am I watching my mom cry again. Nu uh. The tears I've already caused her to shed were more than enough.

Once outside, I breathe in the fresh air and hustle to the shed. Stopping at the door I strip off my protective wear and shove it back into the plastic tub for next time. Furtively, I look around then strip my shirt and pants off as well, ducking into the shed to avoid anyone seeing the goods. Not that it's too big of a concern, because I went through an obnoxious drunk phase a few years ago and mooned the entire block party. People still won't let their kids near me.

I smile at the memory; it was a great night.

I head straight for the shower to quickly wash off; afterwards, I feed the boys, clean their cages and then finally make it back into bed. Snuggling under my blanket, I reach for my tablet. It's my television, my computer, and my window into the outside world. Eagerly, I flip through the free movie app and settle on something romancy. Watching a movie about a gal who has as many bad things happen to her as I do and keeps a diary—I'm way too lazy—helps mellow me out and puts me in a much better frame of mind.

Yawning, I dig around on the small table beside the bed for my phone and find nothing. I always put it here when I get home. The keys are there, my purse is there. Where the hell is my phone?

With the exception of going into my Mom's house, I retrace every step I've taken since I got home. I find it in the last place I expected—Willis's cage. I honestly don't remember it being on me when I cleaned his cage, but I've put my keys in the freezer before too. He predictably bites my hand when I reach in to get it, hard enough to hurt, but not enough to bleed and then promptly shits on the phone.

There are days I sorely regret getting this bird, and this is one of them.

As I'm cleaning the phone the best I can, I swear he's cackling at me from his cage—I latch the door shut in retaliation for his behavior. After spraying some Lysol on my phone, I set my alarm and then crawl back into bed to watch some more romance movies, about things that I'll never experience.

CHAPTER THREE

Birds are indicators of the environment. If they are in trouble,
we know we'll soon be in trouble.
   ~*Roger Tory Peterson*

BY THE TIME the annoying beeping of the alarm saturates itself into my brain, enough for me to realize it means get my ass up, I'm already a half-hour behind schedule. Brushing my teeth while running around wearing only slacks won't win me any beauty contests, but I have to make sure my boys are taken care of before I go anywhere. In this life, there's no guarantee I'll return. This way they have enough food and fresh water until my Mom would come to check on them. I'd like to think it's because I believe in being prepared in life, but that's not why—it's because I'm paranoid about life, and the many things that can go wrong in it.

Death being the ultimate thing. Quite frankly, I'm terrified of it, even knowing it will happen no matter what I do. It's the one guarantee in life; you die. Shivering at my rather morbid thoughts, I rinse my mouth and then attempt to style the unruly hair I inherited from my mysterious father. Mom's hair is so thin you can see her scalp through it. She told me that my lovely, straight as a board, but thick ass blonde hair was a gift from my dad.

Wish he'd left me a million dollars too or maybe a picture of his unknown face.

That part of my existence is a big old mystery that she refuses to talk about. Only explanation I ever got is that he died in the war and there was no body. I suspect she's lying— more than suspect really, but I have yet to look online to see if it's true. A part of me is afraid that I'm some drunken night's result, and that like most of the world, he doesn't want me either. As far as my Mom goes, I would never think to judge her for it, but being the *result* of it... is an entirely different matter.

Hell, a few of the kids in school used to tease me and call me a witch. There is a rumor that my Dad, whoever the fuck he is, was a Wiccan or some shit. I believe that more than the war hero story Mom concocted. Some of the books he left behind are about the occult and witchcraft; they fed into plenty of childhood fantasies, that's for sure. As a kid they were the only comfort I had on days that were for 'Dads' in school, in life. I grew up in the eighties and nineties, when people were stupidly judgmental about kids born out of wedlock. Not just to the parents either.

Not anymore, thankfully.

Meeting my reflection's green eyes in the mirror, I lightly smack my cheek. What is wrong with me? Why am I thinking this depressing shit right before I go to a job interview? I can dwell on it after they refuse to give me a job, and I come home to no food, with only my birds for company. I can really wallow then, get all down in it and give it a good snuggle. Of course, after that I'll cry myself to sleep then wake up and do it again another day. Rinse. Repeat.

Giving up on my hair, I twist it up in a relatively neat bun and slide my shirt on. There's an oil stain of some kind on the left side of the front, which is a prime demonstration of how luck tends to run for me. If it can go wrong, it does. Digging around in my clothes I find a light jacket and put it on. It hides the stain, but makes me sweat. Fall is almost here, so the days are summer-hot, and the nights are cold. This morning is supposed to be in the high eighties and I'm wearing a wool jacket. With a grimace I grab my deodorant; I manage to contort myself enough to get extra on without getting it on the shirt.

Looking once again in the mirror, I grab the small bits of makeup I own and try to turn my face into something presentable. I have a rather round face, and when my cheeks aren't hollowed out from weight loss, it's a bit pudgy. My cheekbones are high, and it makes my eyes slant a little upward on the outside. I don't have the nice thick eyebrows that everyone and their mother sport nowadays. They're a bit patchy, and if I wasn't pressed for time, I'd try to draw some on my face to look a bit better than the mangy ones I have now.

Unfortunately, eyebrows take way too much time, most of which I spend wiping the shit off and starting all over again.

My gaze moves on, my nose is wide and relatively flat, and even though my upper lip has that little bow to it, I still think they're too disproportionate. The top lip is a bit thin while the lower one is overly full. My jaw is too pronounced for that delicate look that's so popular. Mom has it, but I feel like I look a bit square jawed with mine. The slightly round chin doesn't help either. The only feature I feel like I have that's worth a crap is my eyes.

I mean, I'm not the ugliest thing ever created, I've even been called pretty a time or so in my life. I just don't see myself that way. I can't see anything, except my flaws. The curse of being a woman is that we're always harder on ourselves than anyone else.

With a few swipes I put on the last of the concealer, then add a touch of mascara and lip gloss. Satisfied that this is the best I can do, I grab my purse and portfolio and head out the door, right into a rainstorm.

"Oh, this is just freaking great!" I gripe at the cloud filled sky. Thankfully, I have enough sense to keep an umbrella hanging next to the front door. Grabbing it, I open it up and make a mad dash to my car down the street. The bag halfway held on the driver's side, but the passenger side is a loss because I forgot to put another bag on it. There's a puddle of water in the seat and on the floor. Nope, not going to get mad, I have interviews today, which means potential jobs. Can't get mad and ruin the mood for the entire day.

Turning on my car, I let it sit and warm up, ignoring the squealing fan belt. Pulling out my cheese sandwich with crunchy crusts, I wolf it down while putting the address of the first interview in the GPS of my phone. Fortunately, it's not that far away and I won't be late to it, if nothing else gets in my way. Wiping the crumbs off myself I toss the garbage in an old store bag and lock on my seatbelt. Taking a deep breath, I put the car in drive only to stop immediately. The windshield wipers aren't working.

Glancing at the time on my phone in the cup holder, I grit my teeth and grab the towel out of the backseat. Wipe. Wipe. Look to make sure I'm still on the road. Wipe. Wipe. Double check for traffic. After an exhausting fifteen minutes I arrive at my destination. Parking across the street—so they don't see the car—people are weird about shitty cars too, I pull out the umbrella and run across the street.

The crowd of people inside, most of whom look way better than I do, all turn as one to look at me. I'm not too late, but I'm close. As I walk to the only vacant chair in the room, my shoes squeak and slosh on the linoleum floor. I step lighter but the noise increases. Giving up, I roll with it sign in, then head to the chair. At least I have a few minutes to gather my composure.

Right as my butt is getting ready to hit the seat, the door across from us opens and a stern looking woman says, "Miss Riddle, we're ready for you now."

You've got to be shitting me.

Knowing that this is doomed, I stand and attempt to smile at her, as I walk in my loud shoes towards her. Her eyebrow raises, but she doesn't say anything, although she does flick a gaze at my feet.

Well, at least my face doesn't look like stretched rubber.

Forcing myself to not stare at the trampoline tight skin of her face is harder than I expected. Someone has had some work done, often. I look past her as we walk into the small conference room. The gentlemen sitting at the table give me almost identical dismissive looks as I sit at the chair set up alone to face them. The minute they laid eyes on me I was put on their 'do not hire' list. I'm familiar with that look, I get it often enough. This is a job I'd probably be miserable at anyhow, yeah?

That's what I'll stick with, it hurts my pride a little less.

The one to the left, with a bit of brown hair tufting up on top of his head, glances down at the paper in his hand and says, "You've had a multitude of jobs in the last year. Can you explain why you change jobs so often?"

There's that big question, the one I always dread a little. There have been twelve jobs in the last year, no joke. I was fired from every single one of them. Taking a deep breath to say the truth, or at least as much as I can tell someone I'm doing a job interview for.

"I seem to find myself in temporary positions quite often," I say, trying hard to keep the disappointment out of my voice. No matter what I tell myself, I actually want this job. This job would've required me to think and potentially use part of my expensive and useless education. Albeit a tiny part, mostly typing, but still something. I peek down at the paper I'm gripping in my hand and see the next interview is in half an hour. I guess it's time to move this one along then.

"It says here you were terminated, from all of them," he says. That's what I get for being honest.

"Yes, sir."

"Behavioral issues?"

"No, sir." I start listing off the various reasons for the more recent terminations, truthful about them even though I try to make them sound a fuzz less bad. I skip over the ones that make no sense whatsoever. There's no point in sharing those.

There is a resounding silence for several seconds before he clears his throat and continues.

"Do you have any business attire?"

Even though I'm wearing business clothes. I swallow the words that want to lash out at him for his petty insults, and attempt to smile I answer, "Yes." I have nicer clothes; they're in my Mom's house, and probably completely covered in cat hair at this point. Well, maybe I don't have any nicer clothes.

"We'll put together a few scenarios and you answer them to the best of your ability." Oh, look role play, how fantastic. "If John, your immediate boss, borrows your creative idea for an emergency client meeting, what do you do?"

Seriously?

The first answer that pops into my head is not a nice one,

but it's how I'd probably respond in that kind of bullshit situation. The 'scenario' does give me immediate insight into the kind of company this is. I'm not even sure why they're continuing this farce; we all know they're not hiring me. For the moment I'll play along, it's raining outside, and I still have fifteen minutes.

I give them the answer they want to hear, "I would make the decision that's best for the company overall." Fuzzy Head's eyebrows shoot up, I surprised him. I love doing that to people. Each of them makes a mark on their papers and Fuzzy continues.

"John has an emergency lunch with a client and he's misplaced his wallet. Since it's a high profile client John borrows your wallet from your desk without your permission. Keeping this client is a top priority. What would you do?"

Good interviewee has left the building. "Are you shitting me right now?" blurts out of my mouth. Yeah, she's definitely gone. "First, you're making it okay for people's ideas to be stolen, now their money can be stolen too? What kind of crooked ass company is this?"

"Miss Riddle!" Stretch Armstrong exclaims without any part of her face moving in response.

"People like you are the reason that so many good people end up at the bottom holding you up. Lazy fuckers," I grumble, climbing to my feet. Without another word I walk out of the room, through the waiting room full of hopeful looking applicants and I feel a bit of pity for them. It doesn't stop me from going outside in the rain and straight to my car.

My wet car—the bag fell completely off the driver's side window. Sitting in the puddle that is now the seat, I ignore the cold water seeping into my pants and making its way merrily down my legs and up my back. I hit the steering wheel a few times with my hands until I feel a bit better.

Why did I let my mouth run off? Why? I don't think I'd have gotten the specific job I interviewed for, but maybe the janitorial one or something. No one cares about the people who clean up after them, but it was one of my favorite jobs. Until someone accused me of stealing their car... yes, their car. Turns out they forgot where they parked it, but the place still wouldn't hire me back, said I was untrustworthy. To this day I can't figure out how I was the one accused when I didn't leave the floor the entire afternoon. I even skipped lunch that day to finish up my set of rooms.

I have a job jinx.

A gurgle from the area of my empty gut reminds me why I need a job so much. Food, the whole 'gotta eat to live' thing. With a sigh, I rest my forehead on the steering wheel. Whether I want to admit it or not, I'm fully aware that I'll give in and ask my Mom for help before allowing myself to starve to death. There's pride and there's stupidity. I fall into both categories, but in the case of starvation I'll give up pride in a heartbeat.

Just not yet.

Briefly, I sit there feeling utterly miserable until I get it together enough to wipe my face with a tissue and get out of the car. The rain has stopped, leaving the world wet and a bit foggy. Looking around me, I take a few seconds to admire the leaves that are turning the orange of an open flame. To be a bit awed by the way the water is slowly dripping off their pointed tips. As I'm watching this beautiful little miracle of nature, I see something that I thought I'd never see—a shiny black feather floating towards me. The green tint to it indicates that it belongs to a crow and the instant the feather-grabber inside of me wakes up, I need to have it. Ignoring the puddles that I step in on my way towards the rarity, I hustle to try and be under it when it gets close enough for me to grab.

Smiling, because finally something good is happening to me, I hurry a bit faster. The cacophony of screeching tires and tearing metal bring me around to face my car. By the time my brain registers what my eyes are seeing, the delivery truck has slammed into my Herbette. In shock I stand there and stare with my mouth gaping open. With a metallic crunch the truck backs up and my car, that's up on two wheels on the passenger side, hits the ground.

What in the ever-living fuck?!

The driver of the truck staggers out of the door with blood dripping down his face. The reaction I have is not the one I expected. Immediately filled with concern, I run to him and snag a tissue out of my bag to wipe the blood that's dripping into his eyes from the cut on his forehead.

"Are you okay?" I ask softly, dabbing at the small cut above his right eye.

He's young, probably no more than twenty-five, and he looks scared to death. His deep brown eyes are wide with fear and probably shock. When he opens his mouth to speak, he makes a bunch of garbled noises instead then frowns.

"It's okay, that's my car—she was due to retire anyhow," I say way more calmly than I feel. "I do think you need to get this cut looked at, head wounds are weird things," I say while waving at the blonde woman standing on the sidewalk with her camera on us. "Call 9-1-1." I mouth at her and keep muttering calming words to the man in front of me.

After a while, his shaking stops and he leans back against the side of his truck. Thankfully, the ambulance and police come before all the anger building inside of me decides to come out. Now that I know he's okay my emotions are reaching the boiling point. Giving Herbette a look of mourning, I begin to cry. Poor Herbette is completely smashed in on one side, and I know there's no fixing her.

The black feather flutters down and lands right on the

back of my hand, perfectly balanced and beautiful in its multiple colors. It's in that second I realize, this feather saved my life. If I hadn't been chasing it, I'd be as squished as my poor car. With an unsteady hand I pluck it up and wrap it in a tissue. I have a hard-sided glasses case in my purse specifically for these types of situations. Focusing on this task is the only thing that keeps me from breaking down and becoming a complete blubbering mess.

After getting my statement, the cops start their investigation process. I step back and let them do their thing, fighting the urge to kick the truck a few times. I'm glad there wasn't a barrage of questions, because my brain is a bit foggy and the idea of having to think too hard makes me sick to my stomach. So does looking at my poor car.

This is the final nail in the coffin of me becoming a stripper. I've tried to avoid it as long as possible, but I've missed the only other interview that I might have actually gotten hired from.

While I stand there—accepting that I'll be wearing a lot of glitter baby oil and thongs—staring at the train wreck of my morning, the driver is taken away in an ambulance. He's going to be fine, but his company wants him checked out in case. The representative that came out made sure that I have his insurance information in my numb hands. They're paying for everything, but the process will take time they said, so not even a rental car will be provided. That means my insurance will have to temporarily cover it. The tow truck pulls up to take away what's left of my car. It feels like that's what's left of my life, too. Hurriedly, I dig anything I need out of it. My gym bag that's tucked under the seat, some keepsakes that I can't replace and the paperwork.

Then my car is moving away, on the back of a flatbed truck to become another crushed square of metal in some far away junk yard.

The harsh caw of a crow pulls me from the tunnel of blackness that I see in my near future. Frowning, I turn to the trees behind me and find it sitting on the edge of a branch, its head cocked to the side and eyes on me. A foreign urge to move and see if it really is looking at me causes me to step to my left. Unerringly, its head follows me. That's weirdly cool.

"Is this your feather, girl?" I'm not sure what makes me ask it, but who cares if anyone sees me talking to a bird, I do it all the time. Another harsh caw and it hops down to the bench directly in front of me. Cawing again it lifts into the sky and then circles around me, so close I swear I feel the brush of feather tips on my face.

I'm completely nuts in thinking that the damn thing wants me to follow it. Standing there debating it, the first drops of rain fall on my upraised cheek. The noise the circling crow makes this time resembles laughter. Snarky bird. Fine, let's top off a crazy day by following a bird through the streets. As if sensing my decision, the crow leisurely takes off west of me, towards the outskirts of town.

With a sigh I follow, what else can I do?

FOLLOWING the mysterious crow is an adventure, that's for sure, and every time I fall behind she—because it feels like a she—circles back around to get me. Onwards we walk through the town's outskirts, weaving in and out of the wooded areas like we're walking in a maze. To a bird, maybe we are. Looking down on all of us human rats in our miserable mazes of life. Walled in by—*Oh, Jesus shut up, Mel.*

Smirking at the exasperated tone of my 'common sense voice,' I can't help the smile on my face as I follow my new companion. Depression has been my friend for so long, that it's nice to think that maybe for a little while—especially after what happened today—I can feel a different way. Do something other than worry about tomorrow.

Watching her circle above me, then swoop down and land on a stone pillar pulls my attention to the building the pillar is in front of. It's a right creepy place, I can't deny that. The walls are almost a cathedral color brown, with stone columns at each corner and an arch as a doorway. I'm pretty sure there are stone gargoyles on top of the building as well. They look like any other stone gargoyle you see on a building, except these are smiling. A tall black cast iron fence guards the front of it with a bit of a saggy look to it. This place has a definite aura of gloom to it, but that doesn't matter to me.

What does matter is the now hiring sign in the window.

Looking back at the crow I ask, "Did you bring me here because I need a job?" Her answer is that laughing caw.

Now I'm back to the beggars can't be choosers. Patting my wet hair down as much as possible, I straighten my damp jacket as I stroll through the open gate with a lot more confidence than I'm feeling. I mean, come on—the bird's feather saved my life and then she brought me here—something miraculous is going to happen. Hopefully, it's not a plane falling out of the sky onto my head. Or a nuclear bomb or a world-destroying comet that no one saw until ten minutes ago.

TV has made me super paranoid about the impending end of the world. I even have a zombie apocalypse plan, written down and everything, if this gives any idea of what level I'm on with it.

Pausing at the front door, I take one last look at the building that's an absolute b-rated horror movie scene in the making, and go in.

CHAPTER FOUR

Some tribes of birds will relieve and rear up the young and
helpless, of their own and other tribes, when abandoned.
  ~*William Bartram*

THE FIRST THING I notice is that the outside and the inside
don't match at all. The walls inside are an awful puke green
with shit brown diamond shapes, on them. The scheme and
décor are straight out of a seventies sitcom that I remember
watching as a kid. It clashes with the floor that's blindingly
white, and not a single mark or pattern mars its eye piercing
uniformity. Every time I look down at it, I can see my face
clearly reflected. Whoever cleans this place does one hell of a
job. I hope they pay them well, and I also hope that if this is
the job that's available, they don't expect me to be this good
at it.

A small curl of dread flutters through my stomach. I have

no idea what this job is, my brain semi-deserted me while I followed the crow here. Christ, I followed a bird here. My steps falter, as I lean a clammy hand against the ugly wall. What in the world possessed me to pursue a bird like it's a reasonable thing to do? The shock of everything?

Maybe it's the fact that you never do anything fun, Mel.

There's that inner snarky voice again, minus the logic this time. The fact that it's telling the truth doesn't change that I still followed a bird around without questioning it. Straightening, I wipe my sweaty palm on my wet pants and say the most important phrase I've said today.

Fuck it.

Eyes on the door ahead of me I ignore my noisy shoes and the fact that I'm scuffing up their floor. I hike my purse higher on my shoulder and when I get to it, open it without turning around to run like I want to. Inside of the room is a massive amount of potted plants and a single desk. Seated at the desk is a severe looking lady with her blonde hair pulled up into a loose bun. She's somewhat normal looking considering what the rest of this place looks like. However, the look of shock on her face and her gaping mouth make me question things a bit.

Clearing my throat, nervously I say, "Hi, are you still hiring?"

Like a fish gasping for breath out of the water, her mouth opens then closes. After doing this several times, it closes with a snap. She attempts an awkward smile that resembles a grimace more than anything. Straightening the papers in her hand with a tap on the top of the desk she stands and smooths a hand down her tan skirt.

"You can see me?" she asks.

Biting the inside of my cheek, I fight to keep my face straight.

"Uh, yes?" I say it hesitantly, not sure why I wouldn't be able to see her.

"Well, then. Yes, we're still hiring." With a lot more confidence she sits back down in her chair and waves for me to come closer. Acting as if she hadn't been gawking at me seconds before and asking me if I can see her.

"Can I ask what the position is?" I ask.

Her blue eyes, bright in her pale face, pin me to the spot. "The position is several rolled into one. A dietary aid, a housekeeper, and a nurse aid just to name a few of the tasks. It's a hard job, is this something you can do?"

I nod at her, unsure of what will come out of my mouth if I open it.

"Fantastic. You're hired."

Wait, what?

"Just like that?" I can't help but add, "I didn't tell you my name yet." She smiles and hands me a stack of papers and then rustles around in her desk drawer. She gives me a brown bag with what feels like clothes in it.

"It doesn't matter; you're perfect for the job." I think the smile she gives me is supposed to be reassuring but fails miserably. "Be back here at four p.m. sharp for your first day of work tomorrow. You work twelve-hour shifts five days a week and will be adequately compensated."

Wow, that's a lot of hours but hours I need.

"How much per hour?"

"Does twenty-five sound fair to you?" Twenty-five? Good God.

"Did you just say twenty-five dollars an hour?" I ask stupidly.

"Fine, thirty-five."

"Benefits?" I squeak out, biting the inside of my cheek to keep from repeating her words again.

"Full coverage. You'll be provided a card tomorrow, and

the benefits are effective immediately. I suggest you wear the uniform in the bag. Our patients tend to be messy."

"Patients?" Crap, this is some type of hospital?

"Yes, this is an asylum, hum—er, girl. Now, be here on time tomorrow." Feeling dismissed I turn and walk back down the pukey colored hallway. Once outside I look around and notice the hiring sign is gone. Creepy building, yes. Crazy house, yes. Thirty-five bucks an hour, yes. It takes everything I have not to jump up and down in excitement.

The caw of the wonderful bird who brought me here pulls my gaze upward.

"You're freaking awesome!" Smiling, feeling like the weight of the world is no longer pressing on my head I turn and begin the long walk home. I don't even care when it starts raining again.

AN HOUR LATER, I care a lot about the rain. My clothes are sopping wet, and my shoes are now in pieces, I lost the sole off one a half-mile back. The worst part is I still have around two miles to go. Thankfully I made good time this far, and I've at least had a companion for the walk. The crow is still flitting around somewhere, calling out to me occasionally from the trees.

The papers the secretary gave me, or whatever her title is, are tucked inside the gym bag and under my shirt as protected from the rain as I can make them. I fight the urge to check, which will surely get them wet, and make myself keep walking. My purse is tucked under my armpit and will remain there until I can get out of the rain. My phone is gripped tightly in my hand with my sleeve over it. Thankfully, I had enough brains to get a mostly waterproof cover for it when I bought it. The cover cost more than the phone, but it paid for itself a long time ago. I drop my phone all the time, especially on my face when I'm trying to read. I'm not exactly the most coordinated person when it comes to some things and the more protection I can give it the better. It's not like I can afford to replace things every month.

Well, I might be able to if I can keep this job. Because thirty-five bucks an hour! The first paycheck will be more than I've made in a month, no, more than that at some of my other jobs. Even more really. It'll be enough to fill my small fridge with groceries and get the boys some snacks. Maybe I can also get them that new combination cage? Hell, I could buy a car. The thing saving me now is I can take the bus until I get one.

My heart sinks as my great idea dies a quick death. Whenever Herbette wouldn't start, or I was out of gas, I would just borrow Mom's bus pass that she never used. Which means I can do one of two things. I can sell a kidney, or I can ask my mother to loan it to me. Also, ask for some food. I need to be able to eat. That's three things, not two.

Ugh, I'm such a bad daughter.

The caw of the crow pulls me out of the hole of 'I'm screwed' and to the larger-than-normal bird above me. I'm guessing she's someone's pet, she's too acclimated to people for it to be otherwise. I'll look in the lost pet ads when I get home; not that I haven't thought of keeping her around if she'll let me but if she belongs to someone—I'll do the right thing and make sure she's reunited with her owner. I'll deal with that when I get to it.

Thankfully, the rain has finally let up so now she's flying above and slightly in front of me, instead of hiding in the trees. Smiling, I realize that I need to give her a name, something that suits her. Such a clever bird deserves a name, even if it's a temporary one. The first name that pops into my head is Morrigan, but I discard it. It doesn't feel right. I love reading mythology and folklore; seeing how people once thought about the world has always intrigued me.

Most mythology ends in tragedy and one such story involving a crow jumps to mind: Koroneis. For a time before the owl, she was a short-lived companion for the Goddess Athena. However, Koroneis doesn't quite fit her either. Athena strikes me as a better choice, so that's what I'll call her.

"What do you think of the name, Athena?" I ask out loud —that caw of laughter echoes behind her. That's settled then; she likes the name.

As I pass the sign with the name of our housing development, Dark Meadows in faded golden letters, I can't help but exhale in relief. I'm almost home, thank God. Today has been the strangest day ever, seriously, and I've had some weird days. My car was smashed by a truck, I followed a crow to a creepy building that ended up netting me a job, and then I walked all the way home in the rain.

Yeah, totally fucked up day but at least one thing turned out successful. Smiling at the absurdity of it, I see my Mom too late to stop from bumping into her.

Shit. "Hey Mom." The look on her face tells me some type of lecture is incoming which sucks because I want to get out of my wet clothes and destroyed shoes. After I feed the boys, I plan on curling up with a book and my empty stomach.

"I was worried sick about you! The insurance company of the truck who hit you called to let me know that the car would be totaled out and they'll be giving you full compensation. What the hell happened Mel?" She has her arms crossed, and her brown eyes are now full of the ire that used to spell doom for me as a kid. Shifting nervously from foot to foot I mull over what to tell her. The look on her face softens, and she gently grasps my elbow.

"When is the last time you've eaten?" The concern in her voice is thick and my undoing.

Tears immediately start pouring out of my eyes, the whole emotional crier thing kicking in, and I manage to get out, "I borrowed some cheese and bread and had a sandwich this morning." I can't lie to her, not when she's looking at me like that. "I was chasing a feather when the truck hit the car, so I didn't get hurt," I say in a rush. "Oh, and I got a job too."

I'm pretty sure she almost rolls her eyes at me. I see the beginning of it before she blinks.

She doesn't miss a single details as she looks at me from head to toe, "Go inside and get cleaned up, I'll order you some take-out," she says, and my growling stomach loudly answers her. "Mel, you have to stop having so much pride. It's going to starve you to death." Lightly squeezing my arm, she turns away and walks into the house. Staring after her a moment, I frown. She gave in way too quickly and I know it's not the snotty tears, those have been a regular thing my entire life—I'm pretty sure she's immune at this point.

Wait, did she offer to get me take-out?

The cry of Athena close by pulls me out of my stupor and I hurry to unlock the door and head inside. The boys put up a ruckus as I kick off my shoes and socks at the door and slip on the dry, comfy slippers. Comforting them, I tell them about my day as I take care of their food and water while unlatching their cages to let them out to run around a bit. Thinking of Athena, I cross to the only small window in the building. Opening it, I place some bird seed on the sill and call for her.

The boys can't get to the window, so I'm not worried about them getting out.

Needing to be warm and clean I take a quick shower and bundle up in my worn but comfortable pajamas. I grabbed my phone and charger, plugging them in to charge while I read. I curl up on my inflatable bed and merely lay there a minute enjoying it. When Athena lands on the sill with a flutter of wings, I give her a look, and she makes that laughing caw then proceeds to ignore me to eat the seed.

The boys all hop towards her, stopping on the closest rope across the room to huddle together and silently stare at her. In the wild, she'd eat them, and maybe they know this given the way they're all posed like a group of gawkers. Their beaks are even hanging open in shock. Unable to help myself, I snap a picture of them with my phone. This is one of those moments in life that you can't reproduce and want to remember forever.

The knock at the door makes me jump. Laughing at my own reaction, I climb out of my snug nest and open the door with a smile of anticipation on my face. I love Chinese food. It's probably my favorite food and my mouth waters from the thought of eating it. A lot of it. The sight on the other side of the door rips the smile off my face. My Mom is standing there holding a paper bag—which contains my food and an envelope—and with the other hand, she's holding up an old bicycle, the one I had when I was a teenager.

"Mom?" I ask.

"Here's your food," she says, handing me the bag and the envelope in her right hand. Frowning, I take them both and look apprehensively at the bicycle. I'm not much a bicycle person—I wasn't as a teen, and I'm still not one now, but it doesn't take a genius to know why she's dug it out of the basement either.

She plans on me riding the thing to work.

"I thought since you don't have a car until they send us the check to get you another, you might want to ride your old bike. It's reliable and doesn't require anything but your legs to use it."

I sit the food bag and envelope down on the counter

crossing my arms. I look at the rusted, flat-tired mess, and with a sigh, I say, "Mom, it's broken and has been since I was fourteen."

With a small wrinkle between her eyes, she looks at the bicycle as if it's the first time she's seen it. I watch the realization crawl across her face and with a light blush on her face she smiles at me in apology. At that moment I can see the true beauty that once made her the talk of the town. Honestly, she's still beautiful but the life she's led hasn't been kind to her, and her face shows it. Guilt beats me over the head.

I step forward to take the piece of junk from her, wheeling it to the side of the shed where I lean it up against the wall with the full intention of never moving it again unless it's going to the scrap yard.

"I appreciate the thought Mom, but it's out of commission entirely. I'll walk or take the bus."

Her lip curls up in distaste. "Isn't it several miles?" I shrug, deciding not to clarify. The walking will be good for me; lord knows I don't do enough of it. "Mel, why are you always so stubborn?" I shrug again.

"I got it from you," I mumble. Abruptly she laughs, and the tension between us evaporates. I need to get over being weird around her because I feel like a loser. It's not her fault I feel that way. "I'll be okay Mom. There's no reason for you to worry. Hopefully, I can keep this one and move out on my own."

"Mel, why don't you move back into the house?" Oh, the dreaded question. A discussion she's attempted to have with me many times, and one I always—barely—manage to avoid having. Going by the determined look on her face I'm not sure I'll avoid it this time.

"Mom, the cats, and my allergies don't get along." Which is nothing but the truth, just not all of it.

"Mel, I know what my house looks like," sadness fills her pretty brown eyes. "I admit I only see it sometimes, but I know it's there. I just... I can't seem to find it in me to change it." Patting her arm, I try to give her a reassuring smile.

"As long as you're happy Mom, that's all that matters," I say wanting to get the sadness off her face. There's no need for me to say anything about it, she knows, and the idea of humiliating her doesn't please me at all. I might hide from her, but I love my Mom, more than anything. I simply don't know what to do about her... habits.

"Mel, you're such a good girl. Now, enjoy your food and don't go hungry again." She pats my arm and steps forward to embrace me. "I'll call the insurance agent tomorrow to see if they'll give us the money until the company responsible for this fiasco pays up. God knows I've paid them enough money over the years. They can hustle it up a bit. Get a good night's rest, love you blondie." With a smile replacing the sadness in her eyes she turns and heads back into the house. I watch the cats greet her when she opens the back door, and her lips part in a smile as she shoos them back inside. The love I feel for that woman makes my eyes burn.

With a full heart and a growling stomach, I shut the door, wipe my wet eyes, and turn to the food on the counter. It's then that I decide to open the envelope, not truly surprised when I see the three crisp hundred-dollar bills. My first instinct is to take it back to her, but we've played that game before. We'll play a game of back and forth, one she always wins. I've found money in pretty much every place that she could stash it. This time though I will take it without a fight and my first paycheck I will pay her back. I'm surprised when I find the beat-up bus pass as well.

She knew I wouldn't use the bike.

The sick, hungry feeling I'm having for the take-out that I can smell, makes me realize that having pride isn't the same as having a full stomach. To work I need energy, and for energy I need food. Without this money that's something I'm most definitely lacking.

Gah, all this angst is ridiculous.

Mentally and physically shaking myself, I grab the single plate I own along with some silverware and settle down to eat. The boys, still fascinated with Athena, ignore me and continue to stare at her like they've never seen another bird before. Athena however, is not so enthralled with them. With a hoarse whisper of a caw, she hops further into the house and comes to rest next to me on the back of the clothes rack. Turning her head to the side, she studies the food on the fork that's half-way to my mouth and then looks me dead in the eyes.

Amused, I hold out the fork and let her have some. She delicately pulls the piece of sesame beef off the fork and gobbles it down. For the next few minutes, I feed her several more pieces and some rice until she settles down on her feet to watch me. Slowly, I eat my share and find myself full before I want to be. The temptation to stuff myself is there, but I'm pretty sure I'll puke all over the place if I do. After finishing the last bite on the fork, I pack it up and place it in the center of the empty shelf in the fridge. I have breakfast now too.

Tucking the boys in for the night I take care of my before bed ritual.

Grabbing the pack of papers and the uniform I was given out of my purse I make a face when I see the awful thing; solid black with a red pocket and red trim around the bottom of the pants. Well, it's better than white. White makes me look like a walking corpse. Wiggling out of my pajamas I try it on and am at least relatively happy to discover it fits, damn near perfectly. That lady has a good eye for sizes. Shaking my head ruefully, I take it off, neatly fold it up, then put it and a pair of clean socks on the counter. Fortunately, I have a pair of sneakers that don't look too beat-up, and with the pants being relatively long they'll cover the fraying on the tongue of the shoes.

Opening the papers, I grab a pen and sit down on the bed to fill them out.

※

SEVERAL MINUTES later after filling out the typical financial stuff, I read the rules for the fourth time. What the shit? Seriously, what the shit? I've never read such bizarre and somewhat ridiculous rules for a job in my life.

1. No removal of any objects or people from the building. Okay, that one is relatively normal and makes sense.

2. Do not let patients bite you. Okay, that one is a bit odd and concerning.

3. Do not have sexual relations with anyone in the facility. That is an expected and completely normal one.

4. Do not leave your DNA in any room in the facility. Okay, that one isn't normal at all. Is this going along with the sex one, maybe?

5. Do not bring any guests or speak of patients to friends or family. That one makes sense too.

6. Never, ever trust patients. That one sounds ominous as hell but still makes sense.

7. Do not eat ANY of the patient's food. Who would steal food from the patients? That's just crass.

8. Never turn your back on patients. A chill skitters down my spine and I set the paper down. That particular rule gives me a straight-up sense of foreboding. That rule I won't forget.

I guess the question to ask myself, do I really want this job? Obviously, there's some danger involved in it, but the weight of whether that matters or not against the fact that without money I'll slowly starve to death is significantly in favor of the job. With a sigh of resignation, I pick the papers up again and flip to the last page.

If you agree to remain silent about your duties and responsibilities, please place your thumb on the spot indicated.

An ink fingerprint thing maybe? I put my thumb on the paper in the spot marked 'thumb.' Rolling my eyes at my asinine thought that something awesome would happen I start to pull away and find it being held down by an unseen force. A sharp sting makes the digit throb right before I'm released from whatever is holding my thumb prisoner. I cry out in surprise and fall off the side of the bed. Tripping and staggering I manage to gain my feet and glare at the offensive piece of paper.

What the hell just happened?

I stare at the red smudge on my thumb and then look at the dark smear of blood I can see on the document. Did a piece of paper just hold me down and cut my thumb? That's impossible! My heartbeat starts pounding in my head, and my chest feels like someone is bear hugging me. The harsh call of Athena pulls me out of the path of panic that I was steadily going down. Hand on my chest I take deep even breaths and force common sense to rear its head again.

Skittering around the possibility of something that casts a dark light on my family's mental health history, I latch onto something more comfortable to think about in this specific situation. I read somewhere that going without food and solid sleep can make you hallucinate. Food isn't something I've had a lot of so that must be what happened. It's impossible that a piece of paper could hold an adult down. The cut, well—its paper, paper is the devil for cuts, and I've managed to cut myself on it hundreds of times.

Athena hops over to the bed and adds to the surreal feel

of the entire situation by plucking at her skin and then gently pecking the spot where my blood is. Leaning over to see what she's doing I'm floored when I see that she's cut herself and is wiping her blood on the spot. The bizarre, almost glowing light behind it fades, and my blood turns a dark brown. With a cry at me, that I take as her unhappy with my actions, she hops back up onto the top of the drying rack and tucks her head under her wing.

Shaking my head, I grab the papers, careful to only touch the edge of the stack just in case the others want to take their pound of flesh. I tuck them back in the paper bag and set them on the uniform out of reach. Odd or not I need this job, and I can't beat the pay. I need it too much to worry about someone bashing me with their food tray. I can dodge rather well. I used to be good at ducking and weaving. That ability is how I managed to avoid the bullies in school—mostly.

It helps that I have a bit of a temper too.

Crawling back into bed I work on getting rid of the sinking feeling that my life is about to change dramatically. As I drift off to sleep, I manage a small smile of anticipation. The pay is so worth a smack in the head with a food tray, or a possessed piece of paper.

CHAPTER FIVE

HEAR HOW THE BIRDS, on every blooming spray, with joyous music wake the dawning day.
   ~Alexander Pope

THE NEXT MORNING finds me surprisingly rested. Rolling over, I let the small shaft of sunlight rest on my closed eyelids. I've always been a vivid dreamer, and there have been many times that I've gone to sleep just to dream, but last night I can't say I remember having any dreams at all. Different and noticeable, but not that concerning. I was tired. I probably slept super deep.

Stretching, I smile at the nervous flutter in my stomach. There's a bit of excitement there too. I'm one of those people that like working, even shitty jobs. Idle hands are bad for me because I get myself into too much trouble having nothing to do. Opening my eyes, I find myself looking into the black eyes of Athena.

She's on the edge of the bed, her head cocked slightly to

the side, and her beak is open in what I take as a smile. This bird has a shit ton of personality.

"Good morning, Athena." I swear to God her eyes sparkle before she hops off and flaps out the cracked window. The oddness of that makes me sit up; I don't remember shutting it most of the way. In fact, I left it wide open because I was distracted. Hmm. Glancing at the red numbers on the clock next to the bed spurs me into action. I have fifteen minutes to get ready and catch the only bus that stops out here to go into town.

Running around, I brush my teeth while feeding the boys and giving Athena some food as well. My hair goes into a tight bun at the base of my neck and then comes the ugly uniform. Standing in front of the waist length mirror hanging on the wall I make a face at my reflection. Definitely not a flattering outfit, I look like a rectangular piece of licorice. My already pale skin is made even more so, but this color is still better than white or even worse, yellow.

I smooth a hand down the top that feels rough and scratchy like a flour sack. At least the inside of it isn't as bad. My eyes are drawn to the flatness of my stomach. I'm so thin now that the only thing holding my top up is the one thing gifted to me by the boob fairies themselves. D cups. The rest of me is all lean muscle. My hips barely curve out, and the feeling of lacking I had as a teenager tries to wiggle its way back into my brain.

I shove it behind the Wall of Nope. I'm too old to let that bring me down.

With a wave at the boys, I slip on my shoes and grab everything I need for the day then duck out the door. At a full out run, I walk towards the bus stop at the end of the housing development. Thankfully, it's pulling up as I get to the sidewalk. With a wan smile at the driver, I swipe the bus pass at the sensor and climb onto the smelly bus. Most of the seats are taken, so I end up standing in the center to hang onto the pole that decorates the middle of the bus.

Which for a split second reminds me of my employment alternatives if I get fired again. Those thoughts make me grip the pole tighter and be thankful I'm standing there relatively alone. There are times that being around people when I'm nervous I end up fidgeting the entire time or nervously chattering.

No one likes people doing either of those things, especially the ones doing it.

The bus ride is blissfully short, and I'm dropped off at the corner before the asylum. Frowning, I walk towards it. I can't say that I know the name of the place. I don't recall seeing it on any of the papers either. I dig them out of the wrinkled paper bag in my purse to look, discovering I'm right. Not one piece of paper has the name of the company I'll be working for. Not even the tax one.

God, I hope it's not the mob or some other nefarious organization. I'm not sure that a place where they're hiding Jimmy Hoffa's body would be a fun place to work at, but it would be an interesting thing to add to the resume. *'Care-taker for a mob body dump.'* Lots of jobs will hire me based on that alone, right? I only need to dig my job references up out of the backyard. The absurdity of that thought makes me laugh, so when I walk into the long eye-watering hallway, I'm still wearing a smile.

Which fades as soon as I see the dirty look the secretary is giving me.

"You can still see me, then?" she asks.

I nod unsure of how else to answer. Is she a former patient?

"Here are the papers you needed me to fill out." I hand the crumpled bag to her, and she gives its condition a look of disgust. Immediately, she pulls the papers out and turns to the page that has my blood on it. Scowling at it she tucks it away in a drawer then sits back down.

"You get paid once a week, and you can pick your pay up here. We pay in cash only and your first payment will be given out in four days." She's still scowling at me as she speaks. "The gentleman on the other side of the door will give you a list of your duties. Good luck." She waves her hand, and the only other door in the room opens. Nodding while holding my purse to my chest like a shield, I walk towards the dark doorway and step through.

It swings shut and the thunk of it closing echoes in the hallway, making me startle like a ninny, but I quickly shake it off. Even though this place looks flat-out creepy, I can't jump every time there's a noise, or a door shuts. It'll give me a complex. I already have enough of those.

At the end of the short dark hallway sits an older metal desk with a heavy man in a too-tight solid black uniform leaning his elbows against it, looking at his phone. He looks up and spots me. The look of amusement on his face fades to be swiftly replaced with one that looks like he smelled bad milk.

I give him the same look, Mister-Jello-in-a-baggy has no room to think ill of me. None at all. Raising my chin a notch, I walk towards him determined to make the best of this. The hourly rate is spurring me on and giving me quite a bit of courage on my first day.

"So, you're the new one, eh?" The distaste is so thick in his voice I'm surprised it's not dripping off his lips.

Narrowing my eyes, I decided not to point out the giant glob of mustard he has on the front of his shirt. Instead, I say, "Yes, and I was told you'd give me a list of duties." I look down at my purse then back up at him, "Is there a locker room as well?" With a thoroughness that makes me want to throw up a little in my mouth, he looks me over from head to toe. When his eyes get back to my face, I know he's cast judgment and found me lacking—something that in this case, makes me happy. If he doesn't think I'm attractive, he'll most likely leave me alone. Pretty women garner more attention than wallflowers like me.

I can hope.

"This way." He motions for me to follow him and we start a winding trip through the white maze of several unmarked hallways. He walks quickly forcing me to damn near jog to keep up, no sightseeing for me. The end of our journey brings us to a room that looks like it hasn't been cleaned in years. A half dozen beat up lockers line the wall along with a kitchenette that looks like a left-over from the nineteen fifties. The microwave doesn't have buttons on it; instead it has dials and possibly something growing in it. Every counter space, cabinets and the fridge all have that matching moldy looking spots growing on them.

It's a bit shocking after seeing the cleanliness of the area around the secretary.

"There are locks on the lockers, take the key when you choose one. Luckily for you, there's a rule about stealing from the lockers." His face wrinkles up in what I assume is his trying-to-be-intimidating-face. "Food can go in the fridge, but I make no promises that it won't get eaten. Not that you'll need to bring food. You have access to the cafeteria which means you get to eat for free while the rest of us have to pay."

Don't sound so pissy about it, asshole.

"What will I be doing, exactly?" I ask instead of giving into the inner bitch.

"All the shit jobs are yours. Guards don't clean up the mess, not even our own." He smiles like it's a super important job and it makes me want to put his head in the microwave. "You'll be cleaning their crap up too, taking food to them and doing their laundry." The smugness of his voice demonstrates precisely how awful he views the tasks I've been hired to do.

This time a little piece of me had been hoping that I would be working with people, I'd get along with. Maybe ones I could at least have conversations with. Having some work friends might be nice for a change, but I see that so far it won't be happening.

"Okay," I say lamely—his brows that are in desperate need of plucking draw together to form a little fat roll right between his eyes.

"Just okay?" he says, surprise thick in his voice. Was I supposed to ask a man who clearly isn't happy with my presence a bazillion questions?

"Yes," I answer with finality.

"Here is a map of the facility, along with the list of your duties." He hands me a piece of paper with coffee stains on it. "You read the rules?"

I wish the gravity of that question matched the amusement on his face. It's almost like he wants something to happen to me here. This goes into the 'Quit creepy job' side of the list, along with the asshole guard. Right now, the only thing in the positive column is the pay per hour which still outweighs any bad that I've encountered so far—but the day is young.

I can forgive a lot for that pay. That's enough money to live quite comfortably and to pay off the rest of my debt. I'll also be able to get my own apartment, one that I can walk around in more than three feet in one direction.

A gal can dream.

Forcing myself to look down at the map in my hand, I see that the last room number is 111. That's a lot of rooms. "How many of these am I responsible for?" I ask as he's about to turn away.

Facing me again he chuckles, "All of them," he answers, turning away and whistling as he walks the other direction. My first assumption about him is correct. He's a toolbag. "Go to the cafeteria for further instructions, don't bug me about it," he calls over his shoulder as he's clearly abandoning me to learn things on my own.

In trepidation, I look at the map again, and by tracing my finger along the path we took to get here, I locate the room I'm currently at. Following the map, I manage to maneuver myself into the group room. It's an open area, with several old cloth covered chairs placed around small round tables. On each table is a yellow plastic flower in a vase and a stack of blank paper with a single pencil on top of it. There's an old TV in the corner of the room, high enough not to be reached without assistance, that looks like it's at least twenty-years old. The screen is doing that roll thing that I haven't seen since I was a kid, the ancient TV is also wrapped in a wire cage.

Another thing I notice as I walk farther into the room is its complete lack of people. Except for the nurses' station standing against the wall like a bank vault, there's no one, and I'm pretty sure that no one has been here in a long time either. My eyes go back to the nurse station that looks out of place, surrounded by what I think is iron, another peculiar thing for the day. Its occupants are also only visible via a small glass window in the front. The only occupant of the room around that vault looking thing is an eerie silence that makes the sound of my breathing ten times louder than usual.

It also makes me significantly more aware of the annoyed look the nurse is giving me from her throne behind the small pane of glass. I don't miss the fact that there aren't any holes to speak through either. I wonder what happens when she farts in there?

"You must be new," she says, then becomes a total cliché when she picks up a nail file to saw at her bright red fingernails. Or pretending to, at any rate, the file isn't touching them.

"I'm surprised the patients aren't out here... socializing," I mutter, barely loud enough to hear. Of course, she does.

She laughs and says, "You think they're real patients?" She keeps laughing and pretend files her nails, turning the small sliver of attention she gave me away. Unsettled by her statement and knowing that I've been dismissed I meander on towards the cafeteria.

Of course, they're patients. It's a hospital.

It says on this list of duties to give out some food trays at six, some at midnight and then yet again more at four in the morning before I leave. I work five days a week, twelve hours a day. That's quite a bit of time spent here. I'll have to make sure that when I spend time with the boys, it's substantial quality time. The last thing in the world I need is for the other two to pluck themselves bald too. Then I'd have to figure out where to find more bird clothing.

It's not like I can make it, that's a particular skill I don't have.

Crafting of any kind is beyond me. I always seem to make a big mess of it no matter how hard I try. The only thing that I'm relatively good at is time management, or at working through lists and being relatively organized to be more specific. It doesn't matter that I went through a brief phase where I felt like an utter failure because I couldn't cross-stitch. Admittedly, I spent more time bandaging the tips of my fingers than actual sewing, but that's not the point. The *point* is needles are evil, and I have zero skill with them. Or painting, or clay, or drawing. Or anything that involves creative talent.

I even failed one of those mail-in drawing projects that

have the easy connect the dots. Instead of a letter saying, 'good job but maybe next time,' I got one saying I should try a different hobby. A snort escapes me then another. When I picture the result of my attempt at being an artist, it turns into a full laugh. The person who saw the drawing also hilariously wrote that it looked like a zombie penis. My laughter echoes off the empty walls as I work my way towards the smell of food.

Among the myriad of smells, one of which is fried food of some kind, probably chicken, is a coppery underlying scent that I can't place. It smells sickly sweet, almost like decay. Which doesn't make sense. What could they possibly have in there decaying? Shivering from the abundance of things my imagination cooks up, I pause outside of the double doors marked 'cafeteria.' I watch way too much TV because all I can picture now are bodies hanging on hooks in the freezer.

Shaking myself, I take a breath and step through the swinging doors.

The bustle on the other side by a multitude of people in white uniforms going to and from sinks and stoves like human-sized ants is a sudden change from the rest of the hospital that I've seen so far. There is life here in this part of the building. Large ovens line the far wall, and all look full of something or another baking in their pale inner lights. The paranoid person that dwells within me relaxes in the absence of hanging bodies. I bite my tongue to keep from laughing out loud at myself again. I can't believe my weird ass head went straight to that.

"You're the new girl, are ya?" an older woman asks as she stops in front of me.

I turn my full attention to her. She stands a few inches above my five foot two-and-a-half height; her curly, iron-gray hair is peeking out from underneath her netted hat. Her face is round and the lines around her eyes and mouth show a person who laughs a lot. Her eyes are a light brown and sparkling a bit as they size me up like a cow at market.

Yep, there goes my imagination again.

"Yes, ma'am," I answer. Sensing an ally in this woman, I smile at her.

Smiling back, she says, "Good, you look strong enough to do some actual work. God knows the last one didn't. The names, Connie. What's yours?" I tell her. "Come along Mel, and I'll show you what you're supposed to do." Motioning for me to follow her, the first real adventure of my day begins.

꧁

WITH A SMILE still slapped onto my face, I'm handed over to Brett, who's given the responsibility to show me the order we give out trays. I have a good memory, but Connie gave me a cheat sheet, which I'm clutching like the lifeline it is. She said the list would change regularly and there's no way to memorize it. I want to do an excellent job in the hopes I can keep this one for a while. Staying under the radar and doing my job to the best of my ability is the surest way to keep working.

Attention is bad.

Unfortunately, my guide reeks of alcohol and pot and is stumbling through the hallways vaguely pointing at the rooms and mumbling. Seeing that he's not going to be helpful at all, or nice—given his comments on my average looks and how there's no one worthwhile to date in this place—I need all the help I can get. Pulling out the list and the stub of a pencil she gave me with it, I start plotting an efficient way of dispersing the trays since it isn't in the same order as the rooms are. Instead, it crisscrosses, goes up and down and then back again to the beginning. That's not even the strangest thing about it as I read down the list Connie gave me it gets much worse.

Every single patient here has a 'special' diet.

The patient in room one gets an eight-ounce glass of pig's blood mixed with chocolate, six times a day. Yuck. Maybe he's an old guy, and it's some kind of homeopathic diet? Albeit a wholly gross and unhealthy one. I keep reading and discover another patient only gets raw chicken with one broccoli floret as decoration.

Is she teasing me with this menu? Maybe a first day of work joke?

"Excuse me, but are these the things they actually eat?" I ask Brett, hoping he'll answer.

He stops and gives me a bleary-eyed, dirty look. "Yes, what about it?" he says and turns around only to keep mumbling things I can't understand. When he stops suddenly I walk right into his back getting a nose full of stale Cheetos and the tang of the green weed that keeps him hazed and happy.

"You act like they're human or something," he mutters then continues his mumbling journey with me walking behind him slightly confused.

What the hell does that mean? Has he smoked too much today, maybe added a bit to it too? Of course, I act like they're human because we're all humans. He's a peculiar one like the secretary. Maybe they're former patients who are on a work release program? If that's something they have for this type of... facility? That might be just for prisons. Considering I've never dealt with either, I have no idea what's going on. Other than I haven't run into a single person that I'd refer to as normal. Not even Connie.

I need to learn more about this place because my instincts say a lot is going on under the surface here. They also say to cut and run while I can, but my empty bank account nixes that one by overruling it with the life or death need to feed the birds and myself.

My practicality may one day be the death of me.

This thought makes me snort which in turn earns Brett's attention again. He stops suddenly, but this time I manage to avoid walking into him. And his Cheetos and weed smell.

"Is this all a joke to you? This hell hole we're forced to work in?" he snarls, spittle forms on the corners of his mouth as he continues to talk. "I hope they eat you the first day, dumbass."

Whoa, why so hostile? He frowns at me, and I realize I asked it out loud. "Why?" I prompt. I've done nothing to this guy or any of these people deserve to be treated badly. Honestly, I'm quite sick of it happening everywhere I go.

"Because they brought you in instead of offering your job and privileges to more deserving people," he's so bitter I can almost taste it.

His shitty life is not my problem. I shrug and cross my arms waiting for him to shut up and continue walking. I don't understand how there are more privileges for someone who's going to do the work of five people compared to whatever he does. Connie told me I had the hardest job in here, although I'm not so sure of that either.

I'll know by the end of my shift. In fact, I'll know a lot of things by the end of my shift.

CHAPTER SIX

A forest bird never wants a cage.
~Henrik Ibsen

As I MAKE my way through the small, claustrophobic hallways I keep hearing a faint buzzing noise; it sounds like a big fly is flying around in front of me and once in a while doing a flyby of my face. Now that it has my full attention, I realize as it comes and goes it's closely followed by a flicker of color on Brett's back. Determined to see if maybe he has a vibrator in his back pocket, I stare at him until the buzzing sounds again. I stumble when I see what appears.

I should've eaten more today because low blood sugar is making me imagine wings on his freaking back—delicate, pink translucent ones, with little silver veins spidering out. They glow like a neon sign and leave little light trails when they flutter as fast as a bee's wings. While I'm watching they appear and then disappear several times. I've only gotten a few solid flashes of them, but enough to know that they're definitely wings and they're definitely not real. People don't have wings, right?

Maybe the buzzing noise is why my brain is cooking up wings to explain it?

Odd they're pink though, I would've guessed green ones with pot leaf-shaped veins in them or bright orange ones with cheese dust when they flutter. I stare at the back of his greasy head and bite back a giggle. When they flicker into existence again my smile fades. I make myself blink, and they disappear, but my stomach is still queasy from the hallucination now that my moment of levity has fled. Once more they flicker in and out of existence, and again I blink. The only good thing about the imaginary wings is they distract me from the shadow person I occasionally see walking beside me. On the wall. Sideways.

After this, I'm going to sneak a few bites to eat and maybe shut my head in a door a time or two. That will hopefully take care of the whole 'seeing things' issue I have going on right now. If not, then I'll break down when I get home and find a place where I can make an appointment with a psychologist. This type of thing runs in my family and... well, I was hoping to avoid it since I'm thirty-eight and other than a few burps haven't had any other full-blown symptoms. A small hope flickers, for all I know this is some emotional breakdown from stress which would be better than the alternative. They happen to people all the time it happened to my Mom even. It's why she does what she does with the house. The illness that ultimately killed her mother skipped her.

Unfortunately, she's the victim of other mental illnesses; I don't want to end up that way, not if there's a way to head it off. There's no shame in it, but that doesn't mean it's a road I want to walk if I can prevent it from happening, or at least start the treatments before it gets too bad. The nausea in my stomach is enough to bring those dreadful thoughts to a stop. Probably a temporary one but I'll take it.

Brett stops in front of the door marked with a slash that I'm guessing is supposed to be the number one. We circled back to the beginning, and the tour is over.

"The other floors you can figure out yourself, I'm not going up there," he says, turning the knob and opening the door. "Here is the room you care for every single day, no matter what you have to do." That doesn't sound ominous or anything.

The room inside is mostly dark with only a faint light seeping through the heavily barred window. Something inside moves and with shuffling steps heads towards the door. The harsh fluorescent lights from the hallway touch the incredibly fragile looking face of an old man. His blue— no, white eyes... nope, blue again. Under the lights, they seem to be shifting between blue and white. They zero in on me and stay there giving me a spine-tingling feeling of... something. I'm not entirely sure what.

What incredibly disturbing and awesome eyes to have.

They sparkle with amusement as they hold mine, unflinchingly. When he smiles, I gasp, all his front, upper and lower teeth are missing. The exposed gums are shiny with fresh blood, that's also stained around his lips and in rivulets down his chin.

Well, this just got creepier.

"He liked to bite until the doc fixed that problem," Brett says with amusement.

The thought of them doing that to this frail, old man bothers me on every level. What kind of place have I stumbled onto? I make a mental note of it and his room number. I've never dealt with something like that. I'll have to look up what to do or more importantly, what they can do to patients. I mean they used to give out lobotomies like candy. A bit distractedly, fascinated by the old guy I study him. My instincts say he's dangerous, that he's more than he seems. Like an annoying fire alarm, they register him as a threat—but not to me. I'm not sure why I think this, but the surety of it is concrete in my gut.

"Hello," I greet with a hesitant smile. Surprising myself and Brett who looks at me in shock. The eerie man smiles again and slightly inclines his head.

"Hello, beautiful," he says as those eyes of his shine, and he steps back into the shadows. My heart skips a beat, and a feeling of awareness flashes through me like fire. Taking a few deep, shaky breaths through my nose I swallow the feeling that's borderline arousal—ick, he's an old guy—and turn to look at Brett.

"Only cowards do things like that to someone who has no defenses," I growl. It's a vile act in the least, and the fact that it happened should make me walk out right now. But something is telling me not to. My eyes go back to the man in the shadows who I know is watching me. I feel like he *needs* me.

How weird is that? That doesn't make it any less accurate, however. I feel it as realistically as the ground beneath my feet, and for now, I'll heed it. I'll also for sure be making an appointment to get my head examined. I need to, after deciding to remain here after the pink wings and the fact that they pulled out his fucking teeth. All signs point to GTFO. For now, I'll stay.

I might very well change my mind before the end of my shift.

Brett is standing there giving me a somewhat confused look. "You act like you care about them?" he questions.

"Who wouldn't? Look what you did to..." I hook a thumb

towards the man in the room whose name I don't know. The list has room numbers and diets, no names.

"Vale," the old man says softly from the darkness, sending shivers down my spine. I really need to get my head checked; those were the good kind of shivers, and I'm pretty sure he's old enough to be my grandfather. Maybe even my great-grandfather.

A soft chuckle drifts out, and I turn to look at him, frowning. I swear it's almost like the dude can read my thoughts. "Your face is so open, and I've had years of practice reading them," he says in a voice that's incredibly deep for a geriatric Casanova.

Brett grabs my upper arm and forces me to look at him. I grab his hand twisting his last three fingers backward until he yowls in pain and pulls away from me. Now several feet from me he's giving me dirty looks and nursing his sore hand.

"Touch me again, and I'll break it," I say through gritted teeth. All those years of being bullied paid off. Mom put me in Krav Maga classes my freshman year in high-school. I made it all the way to the blue belt before the instructor closed the teaching center. I was his only student, and he couldn't afford to stay open. To be fair, I haven't kept it up but some things you never forget.

I'm not Bruce Lee, but I won't go down without breaking or biting something off. That strangely sexy chuckle comes from the dark room once again. Whipping my head around I look to where I know he's standing.

Do you have wrinkly balls? I ask in my head.

Another chuckle and then he asks, "Are you thinking something naughty, beautiful?"

The bottom of my stomach drops out and I back away from the door. Is he really that good at reading my face? There's no way he read my mind. This place... is so fucking off. A home or prison to a sexy man who looks like he'll crumble to dust any minute and pink winged orderlies. Or a place that pulls out a patient's teeth. The wall stops my backward journey and Vale; he has a name now, starts walking towards me. Smiling his bloody-gummed smile, he looks inhuman. Those eyes that hold me prisoner flash in the light like a crocodile and give me goosebumps.

"No harm shall come to you here, not from any of us," he says lifting his hand towards Brett who freezes in place a look of abject fear on his face. Vale stops a scant foot from me and with a look of pure apology, spits in my right eye. The wash of red swirls across my eyeball and then starts to burn, within a second it feels like it's on fire. Staggering away from him I lift the edge of my shirt to rub it, and the pain only increases.

"What did you do to me?" I demand. Scrubbing at my eye with my shirt. All the fear of what could be in his blood, of what could *infect* me in my voice.

I was nice to him!

"You're on your own new girl!" Brett exclaims, and I hear the receding footsteps as the chicken shit runs the other way. Gradually the burning starts to ease, and I can see out my eye again. Maybe? The world is awash in colors. The hallway is a purple color with smoke or fog swirling at my feet. On the wall small black lizards crawl about, some stopping to look at me in curiosity before moving on.

What. The. Fuck.

"You have to fully see to survive this place because once they realize what you can do, they will stop at nothing to make sure you're in one of these rooms with us." He's speaking from above me, and I discover that I'm sitting on the ground and I have no idea how I got here. When I look up at him, he hands me a white handkerchief. Taking it, I give him a dirty look and wipe my face, wishing that I was near a shower. As I pull the cloth away, I see a smear of blood on it. A lot less than it felt like hit me, still gross though.

"I've lost my fucking mind, haven't I?" Hands covered in paper-thin skin, so soft that I feel like a mere breeze can bruise them, lift me effortlessly to my feet. I immediately step away from him. He spit blood on me... on purpose. He's probably infected me with God knows what. I realize that I'm shaking and cram my hands in the crook of my elbows to hide it. I should walk away, I know this, but well—I need to know if I've indeed fallen off the deep end. Mostly because there's a dragon at the end of the hallway looking at me while she paints her talons.

I'm not kidding.

She's small, about the size of a large dog but unmistakably a dragon; with wings and everything. How I know, it's a she, that's the mystery because the painting of one's nails is not a concrete way to guess. There's just a feminine air about her, I think? God, I hope they give me some awesome pills when they lock me up here because I'm pretty sure I've freaked out and am imagining this entire thing. Wait, maybe I'm already a patient here and I've imagined living in a shed in my Mom's backyard with three birds?

Couldn't my crazy have provided a better fake life than that?

The sharp slap on my cheek pulls me right out of the rabbit hole I'm falling down. Gritting my teeth again, I slap him back, or I try to—once again I get nothing but air. How does someone so freaking old move so fast? A few feet from me he's watching me once again in that reptilian way, a smile on his toothless mouth.

"Welcome to the Nothing. Coming here is something a normal human can't do. You did, which is a testament to your true nature. Your eyes were not opened enough to this world, and that put you in danger," he explains hurriedly, in a loud whisper, his eyes intent on me.

Logic reasserts itself, thankfully. "Okay, I'm sorry—I need to call someone. I'm just the maid; you need the doctor." He rolls his eyes at me. A man that's so old he has jowls just rolled his eyes at me *after* spitting blood in my eye. I turn to walk in the general direction of the main room someone there can deal with this. I clean rooms and feed them. I don't deal with their... issues.

Stepping around the skeleton dressed in striped pajamas staring at me I say, "Excuse me." Then keep walking. I'm all the way at the end of the hallway when I realize what I did. Shit. Vale chuckles again, and I look over my shoulder at him. He's standing there one hand gripping the wall watching me with swirls of shifting colors undulating around him.

My head hurts from my left eye trying to adjust to the new vision of my right one. Wait, what? Covering my right eye, I look at Vale. He still looks a bit odd for an old man, but there's no smoke, no skeleton—no dragon. Colorful flickers yes, but not the full-on movie. Switching eyes, I clench my jaw, all the weird stuff is back. I drop my hand, the eye he spit in is the one I see all this stuff with. If it were drugs, I'd be seeing things out of both eyes, if it were hallucinations, the same.

What else could they be but hallucinations?

"Survive, Melantha. I'll see you at mealtime." With that doom and gloom shit said he ducks back into his room, leaving me standing there with a skeleton who shrugs at me then starts shuffling back down the hallway.

How the fuck did he know my name? Freaked out and with more speed than I should probably be using indoors, I hoof it towards the main room. When I finally get there, I'm huffing and puffing from exertion. I'm pretty sure at one point in time I was flat out running. The nurse looks up from her desk and sneers at me.

"See something scary new girl?" Why does everyone keep calling me girl? I'm almost forty freaking years old.

I open my mouth to tell her that Vale spit in my eye, but something stops me. Maybe it's the way that the skin on her face is fluttering or how the smile she has isn't real at all. It's a smile of confirmation. She knows and is expecting me to rant about monsters. Why does the surety that telling her will put me in danger fill my stomach?

I can't believe I'm letting the warning I got from a tooth-less old man who spit on me affect my judgment, but there it is just the same. "Spider! Big fucking spider!" I exclaim waving my hands around as I turn and walk towards the locker holding my Chinese food. I feel like eating something, it's the only normal part of this day, and I'm determined to have that.

Connie heads me off outside of the lounge.

"Mel, I was told you might be heading this way," she pauses, "Brett said you met Vale for the first time." I look up at her, way up which is funny considering that when I met her earlier, she was shorter. And wow, gossip travels super-fast in this place. That was a whole ten minutes ago.

"What else did Brett say? Anything about him running like a scared little girl?" I say. Connie laughs, and her pose relaxes.

"I figured you were planning on packing up that pitiful lunch of yours and running home yourself," she says giving me a hard look.

"Maybe, I haven't made up my mind yet. I wanted to eat first because the chewing helps me think," I answer honestly and perhaps somewhat stupidly; however, it's nothing but the truth. When I eat, I think while I chew.

"You're an honest one, but you're here because you were

meant to be." She leans forward and pats my shoulder. "Well, I'm not going to let you eat that cold garbage, come along. I have some food you can eat while I get their meals together." Oh, that's right I need to give out trays which means going right back to Vale.

Why does that make me feel afraid and excited at the same time? Seriously need to shut my head in the door.

CHAPTER SEVEN

No bird soars too high if he soars with his own wings.
~William Blake

I STARE DOWN at the ID card that Connie gave me to get onto the third floor. The 'high security' wing she called it and then mumbled something about how they 'couldn't pay her enough to go up there.'

That's reassuring, right?

And the picture on it. I'm not even looking towards the camera. I had no idea when they took it, but here it is in all its glory, gaping mouth and all. I let it fall back against my chest and start pushing the tray cart again. It's a big silver monstrosity that's exactly like the ones you see in the hospitals, but it doesn't look like it'll hold the food for one-hundred and eleven rooms. Connie reassured me it will and sent me on my way.

My job isn't to tell her what to do, in fact, it's the other way around entirely.

As I push the squeaky thing down the hallway, I ignore the colors and critters I see all over the place. A lot like how I overlooked the horns coming out of Connie's forehead, they were petite and cute so other than staring at them—which she noticed—I said nothing. It was hard, too. They were bright green, like nuclear green and had this adorable little curl to them. When I shut my right eye all I could see was her happy face and her hair net—no horns.

I also stuffed my face. With warm, fresh baked bread and cheese that tasted better than any I've ever had before. I'd bet an arm it was homemade right here. The cherry on the entire meal was the tomato soup. Thick and tangy with the right amount of flavor to make my tongue orgasm with the first spoonful. I had to fight the urge to lick the bowl clean, and that's after scraping off as much of it as I could with the spoon. I can still feel it happily sloshing around in my belly as I walk. It's been a long time since food has given me such a satisfied feeling as I have right now. This happy food-zone is a place that I don't find myself too often, and I plan on enjoying it.

Looking down at the list I have taped in front of me on the cart I see which patient gets fed first. The order is haphazard, showing no priority it says very clearly to follow the specific order listed, and that order can change daily—something I plan on doing right because it's my first day and I'm not about to get fired this fast.

I'm still adjusting to this weird hallucination thing I have going on. Yeah, I know that I determined that it wasn't a hallucination but what else can it be? The stuff I'm seeing out of my right eye that's all tinted purple and acid-trippy looking can't be real, so I'm choosing to ignore it. Every single job I've had I've lost for one stupid reason or another, some of which didn't make sense, I refuse to quit this one.

I can't promise I won't get fired sooner rather than later. My getting fired seems to be the common thread. Especially if I keep seeing weird humanoid looking things crawling on the walls with the lizards and spiders. The people though are worse, far worse. When I look at some of the residents, it's like seeing another form superimposed over their human one. I've never gotten drunk on the job before, but I'm seriously tempted. Being intoxicated might help me stick with the determination not to quit and check myself into a regular psychiatric ward—one that doesn't have walls that move.

That's the thing I'm trying to ignore the most, those breathing walls.

The calm that keeps me moving, and doing the job is not something I expect to remain, considering all the shit going on around me. I should have already run from this place screaming at the top of my lungs for the Ghostbusters. Instead, I give the man whose face is a maw of shark teeth his tray. On it is one big bowl of pink squiggly meat, a neatly folded napkin, and a spoon. My stomach protests at what I think it is, well, pretty much know it is. I can't say I've ever seen a brain in real life, but I've seen plenty on the internet and TV, and I'm pretty sure that's what's in that bowl.

Pausing, I stare down at the next tray in my hands. Blinking at it rapidly, I swallow the bile in my throat. The smell of it is enough to make me swallow again just to keep from adding my vomit to his plate of 'spaghetti.' Which has maggots in it and possibly some cockroaches. Live ones. Why this makes me more nauseous than brains I have no idea. They're also something I can't deny seeing, with both eyes. Without looking at the recipient, honestly afraid of what I'll see, I keep my head down and hand them their tray. Quickly, I move onto the next name on the list, swallowing several times to try and keep my stomach from emptying its lovely contents.

When we walked through the first time, all the doors were open and people... ha, people were walking in and out of them freely, but now they're all closed. Yet, I know they're all now standing on the other side watching me so intently that I can feel their hunger.

And the day gets weirder.

I pray to whatever gods are listening for me to make it through the day, so I can get back into the kitchen where I feel somewhat safe, and think. I really need to think again. I need to analyze myself. Yeah, I'm a little freaked out but accepting this... shit so easily is what I need to think about. When I was young, I used to imagine this kind of stuff in vivid, 3D detail. My imaginary friends were toothy monsters and talking krakens. Basically, things like those that inhabit this place.

It's almost like I've come home, how fucked up is that?

As I go about my task, a shiver runs up my spine, and I make myself stare at the floor to keep from looking behind me, where Vale's room is. I know he's standing there watching me. I have no idea how I know, but I do. That gaze of his is like fingers running across my skin with a bit of scary thrown in. The repulsion that's clashing with the attraction is something I know is a result of his age; well, mostly because of his age. The fact that I'm attracted to him in some way makes it all the more creepier and noticeable.

He's a walking sack of wrinkles and ointment; I shouldn't feel anything but the normal sympathy and fear that I feel around senior citizens. Sympathy, because I feel bad for how most of them are treated, and fear because I know I'll be them one day. Also, I don't recall smelling ointment when I stood next to him, more like a sweet, earthy smell. That unique smell you get when you're digging your garden for spring planting and the dirt smells rich and pure. That's the closest thing I can think of to compare it to. I love the smell of freshly turned soil which adds to the mess that defines who I am as a person.

Big ole hot mess.

As I walk around from room to room, I can't help but notice all the pink dragons on parade. And purple. And blue. This sight makes me snort and chuckle a little as I keep walking. Wasn't the cute elephant from that kid's movie drunk when he saw that? My laughter fades when I realize I'm at the first room of this floor and look up right into the amused gaze of Vale. Vale who's looking at me like I should be his on his tray. I'm unsure of whether it's the sexual kind of hunger or gnawing on my leg kind, but it's intense whatever it is. When his eyes brighten and he smiles broadly, showing those bloody gums of his, I get my answer.

Both. Without a doubt.

A wash of confusion makes me pause—out of all the things I've seen today, this is by far the most bizarre one. As I stand there, with a puzzled frown on my face, I hold out the tray containing a large Styrofoam cup of red, goopy liquid which I know is pig's blood and chocolate—with a squirt of whipped cream on top. With another gummy smile, he says, "You're still telling yourself it's hallucinations?"

I shrug, "So?" Do I sound defensive? I'm pretty sure I do. *Great.*

He looks at the cup with a mixture of hunger and repulsion, a strange look to see, but then again, the stuff in the cup doesn't seem all that appealing. Snatching it up, he sniffs it, then tips it up and starts to down it in loud wet gulps, not even stopping when it runs down his chin to soak into his crisp white scrub shirt. He sits the empty cup down on the tray with enough force that it almost causes me to drop it, he burps softly and twists his red-stained lips in disgust.

"If I had real human blood, I would not be in this condition," he mutters.

"I'm sorry, what did you say?" I ask, not sure I heard him correctly.

With a sigh, he pulls another handkerchief out of his pocket and wipes his mouth. The air around us gets thicker, causing my ears to pop. Directly around me, the air shimmers and I swear it feels like I'm standing in a bubble.

"Soon enough you will accept what you see as truth," he pauses studying me, then continues, "I must admit that I do regret that I couldn't take you into this slowly," he says, stepping towards me. Immediately, I take a step back towards the cart away from the hand he's holding out. He makes a face and drops it to his side. Anger burns bright in his eyes as he says, "With human blood, I would return to my true position and get rid of this ridiculous mortal coil. They withhold that privilege from me to keep me weak and at their mercy in this wretched place. Forcing me to remain here, as a prisoner for no other reason than being what I was born to be." He speaks in that calm tone of voice someone uses to talk about the weather or who's winning at football. Not about drinking blood and dying.

"Eventually you'd have seen all of us as we are. It would have simply taken too much time and time is not something any of us have. Especially you, because unlike us, you do not have any gifts to protect yourself. You are far too mortal for the abilities you possess, Mel."

Through my sticky, dry mouth I manage to get out, "What abilities are those exactly?" I have no idea why I'm playing along with this insanity, but my instincts are insisting upon it. As fucked up as they obviously are since I see fantastical things—some of which are kind of cool, to be honest—I decide to listen.

"World walking. It is how you came to be in this place and

how you can see the truth using my Blood Mark," he looks at me much like an eagle looks at a fat squirrel, "Did none of your journey here seem strange to you, outside of me expanding your vision?"

"A bit. I mean the wallpaper in the reception area is hella outdated," I ramble, wishing fervently that my lips would stop flapping.

"The *wallpaper* struck you as strange?" he asks incredulously. If he'd have called me a dumbass right then, he wouldn't have been wrong.

"My family has this," I wave my hands around as I search for the right word, "thing." Great word Mel. "Illness thing." Not much better, Mel. I blow out a breath. "They see things, and then they end up in places like this for the rest of their lives."

"Schizophrenia?" There's the dumbass call out.

"Yes," I answer.

"You don't have that. Although those who carry that badge aren't always mentally ill, humans are too eager to place a label on things. Sometimes they're merely seeing the other worlds layered over their own and are interacting with them on a level that normal humans can't."

Cool explanation aside, why am I standing here talking about seeing things and mental illnesses with an asylum patient?

"This is not an asylum; this is the Unsylum. You need to remember that," he says, clasping his hands behind his back, "An asylum is supposed to offer shelter, safety and support. There's none of that here, beautiful Mel. This place is full of death and pain."

"Am I in danger from the patients?" Why does saying the word 'patients' feel wrong? Why does a small voice in my mind whisper that I should say 'prisoners' instead? Another thing to add to the weird as hell day. One which isn't even half-way over.

"None will hurt you here. It's the ones that run this place that are the threats to you," he answers.

"Aren't they threats to you too?" I have no idea what made me ask, too late to take it back now. Logic keeps trying to reassert itself but at the same time... there's another voice in there that says the logic is my fear talking and not logic at all.

"They think they are," he smiles again and looks so menacing that I almost take another step back. His hand on my elbow stops the urge from coming to fruition. Giving it a soft squeeze, he releases me and steps back.

"You seem so nice..." My mouth moves with the words, but there's no sound.

Somehow, he hears me anyhow and says, "Oh, never think that I'm nice. I killed your predecessor and hers before. And in the event of your demise—which I plan on interfering with—any who come after you and every one of the... *staff* in this building will die." His eyes lighten and begin to glow, as fangs grow into the spaces left from his missing teeth. Long and sharp and stained red with blood. The skin on his face tightens, and a new one emerges that looks monstrous and beautiful at the same time. The presence he exudes, that aura of dominance around him expands, and as I stare, he looks ten feet tall. A chill runs down my spine and raises every single hair on my arms.

When I blink, he's once again an old, stooped man with missing teeth—another hallucination.

"But not me?" Oh, look more words coming out of my mouth that shouldn't be.

"Never you, Beautiful."

Confused by that preference I ask, "Why?"

Why is a good question, like, *Why am I standing here*

talking to him when he said he murdered the person who had my
job before?

"Return later, and I'll tell you more." With those words he steps back into the sudden complete darkness of his room and vanishes from sight. I know he's still there. He's doing that thing where he stares at me from the dark, I can feel it.

With a sigh, I turn back to the cart, ignoring the fact that my hands are shaking like a leaf when I grab the handles to push it. That fear filled logic still exists, and it comes awake with a roar. All this is a symptom of mental illness—that I had hoped to avoid—and quite possibly one that Vale is adding to his delusions, too. It's fucking infectious and I really do need to quit.

Don't I?

He can't possibly be telling the truth, right? Admitting blatantly to murdering someone, hell—several someones, that can't be true?

Mulling this over I head towards the elevator. Stopping at the bent metal doors, I push the button marked two and wait for its arrival. The creaking and groaning coming through the closed doors isn't reassuring me about the safety of the damn thing. Still, this must be done. I don't see me being able to maneuver this thing up several flights of stairs. I'm not even sure the massive thing will fit in the stairwell door. Wherever that is, I don't see one marked on the map.

The doors whoosh open and inside is a surprisingly large space, that is the same pristine white tile that's on the floor. The lights on the ceiling are blinding; I'm dumb enough to look up so now every time I blink, I can see them behind my eyelids. That's too damn bright. There's also a strange buzz in the air, thick and unpleasant. My skin is tingling from it almost like it's trying to get away from it. With a creak, the doors slide shut and the elevator jerks as it starts its slow ascension. Several minutes pass as I stare at the closed doors of the elevator. By the time the doors open and I'm able to hastily push the cart out enough to look back at the death trap, I'm ready to run.

Why did it take over five minutes to move up one floor? It didn't feel like we were moving that slow. Having no choice but to move forward to get things done, so I'm not behind, I move on.

There are guards at the desk at the end of the hallway who look rather nonchalant. A slim, dark-haired man that has pink wings like Brett looks up at me first. The curl of his lip is the first reaction he has to me. Asshole. He and Brett have more in common than those tinkerbell wings of theirs. Maybe that's why they're jerks? The girly wings and too tight uniforms? His dull blue eyes narrow as if he senses I'm making fun of him internally. Other than the wings, nothing about him looks otherworldly. At least the hallucination doesn't give the jerks special looks too. I think it would suck if they looked cool but acted like that. I smile lamely and look at the other one.

The other is blonde and slight, no wings for him, but pointy ears are peeking out of his hair—big crooked pointy ears. He lifts his brown eyes to look at me like I'm rubbish at his feet. No shock there. Other than Connie and the kitchen staff, the dislike from the others that work here is becoming a common occurrence. Not that I'm specifically used to being Miss Popular but still, assholes. This particular one is obviously an elf of some kind, but my imagination isn't being very creative with it. Where is the LOTR theme that I love? The blonde one that is so damn cute you wanna hug him to death with your boobs. Instead, this guy looks like a washed-out former eighties band member who had one bad trip too many. His skin is pale with dark circles under his eyes and sallow looking. His fairy winged partner is no exception. Plus, he looks like he's sporting a black eye on top of whatever illness plagues him. Addiction maybe? Automatically my eyes go to his arms looking for needle tracks. There's nothing and I mentally roll my eyes at my behavior.

Curious that I jumped to addiction.

Deciding to follow my list and ignore the dickish behavior, I start moving towards them. I immediately notice that the hallway grows darker as I enter it. The doors on each room are shut and made from steel. My curiosity gets the best of me so when I stop at the first one I touch it. No, not steel, the surface is rough and smells metallic. Iron perhaps? Why are the doors made from something as antiquated as iron? They're secured with a large lock that looks old enough to be in a museum. The only opening is a slot for trays. Some of which are larger, but so are the items on the dishes. None of the slots are the same size; I swear it's like they tailored the doors to everyone's food.

The higher security here than there is on the first floor is a concern too.

Shaking out the cobwebs in my brain, I start handing out trays. Some stay on the metal shelf on the door, untouched, others disappear immediately. Behind those doors I hear growls and other strange chewing noises as they devour— that's the right word for it—their breakfast. For some reason these noises and the dark thoughts they incite, that *should* be terrifying to me but aren't, remind me of Vale.

What is it about that man that fascinates me?

I don't like admitting it, but it's there just the same. Odd and uncomfortable, it makes me feel conflicted in a sickening way. There's a touch of sexual attraction, but it's not full-blown crawl on him like a monkey kind. Yet, it exists, whether I like it or not. The feel of it reminds me of a simmering pot of water—one that you're impatiently staring at waiting for it to boil. Like there's a missing piece that isn't there yet, which is abnormal for me. I have a type: muscles, and empty heads. Oh, and always losers, that's a thing too.

Vale is a crazy old man in an asylum... *Well, I guess you can't get anymore loser than that, right Mel?*

Shaking my head at the bullshit running through it, I hand out the next tray and ignore the glowing purple eyes looking through the food slot at me—eyes that are the same height as a child. I don't need anything else freaky heaped onto the I-need-to-be-committed-leaf-pile. It's not a secret that places like this have children in them, just not usually mixed in with the adults. Gritting my teeth, I move on. It's none of my business. At least, not on my first day. It can haunt me when I go home and run this entire oddball day through my head, then maybe call whatever authority deals with this shit.

Vale is the other thing I need to figure out because some-thing about him isn't sitting well with me. Maybe it's the way he holds himself that's so very different from his appearance? That brief glimpse I saw, fit him more than the frailty he has as a mantle now. To get down into the meat of it, it feels like I *know* him from somewhere. The familiarity of him is fucking eerie. The desire to step into him and feel his arms around me was sudden and completely freaked me out. So much so that I refused to think about it when I was standing in his presence. Since he can read my face or thoughts or whatever the hell he's doing to guess so well. At least, my insane mind is convincing me he can read it, thinking it's almost the same as telling him.

A sharp pain in my head makes me pause in my steps, but then it goes away just as quickly as it appeared. Christ, I think that was an honest to God brain cramp.

Fuck me. I got issues.

The last tray is passed to its recipient, and I look on my list to guide me next. The third floor that no one wants to talk about or go to, apparently. A good guess tells me that it's probably where they keep the patients they deem 'dangerous.' Probably the trolls and kelpies, right? Snorting, I push the button marked with the number three on the elevator and wait for the grumbling contraption to ding its arrival and open its maw. I only jump a little when it arrives. I'm not a fan of elevators that work correctly and quietly, let alone one that sounds like it's going to fall into the darkness of the elevator shaft with every inch it moves.

I push the cart inside and push the button to close the doors. Leaning against the wall, I wait for the journey upward. I'm assuming it will be as slow as the first time. Pulling my phone out of my pocket takes some effort. This stupid uniform is tight across the hips. I have no signal, but the time says half-past seven. Whoa, it's been an hour and a half since I started this? I need to pick up my pace.

Suddenly, the elevator shakes and groans loudly coming to a jarring halt. Hard enough to rattle the contents of the cart and make me stumble a bit to keep my footing. The door jerks open and the foyer in front of me is damn near dark with only red lights lining the walls. The number three hand-painted on the wall in bright red paint is taller than I am. That's something that sets the tone of foreboding filling my stomach.

With a bracing breath, I start pushing the squeaky cart towards the only door that I can see. Beside it there's a red button, a consistent theme for this floor. I walk around the cart and read the sign above the button.

Push button for assistance, the door is always locked. You enter at your own risk.

Oh, look another dire warning. This place has them everywhere and from everyone. I admit that I still see things with the purple tingeing, everything I see outside of my right eye, but I have yet to be hurt by anyone. No one has threatened me either, and the only person who has 'scared' me per se is Vale. Although, I'm not sure that fear is the strongest emotion he draws out in me.

Which is a mess and of itself. One which I need to sort out once I'm out of the influential sphere of the Unsylum. I push the red button and wait. His words do concern me a bit, the way he put it as a prison or a punishment. I guess from a patient's point of view going to an asylum *is* punishment. Then you throw in them pulling his teeth out. A sharp pain shoots through my head again and vanishes like the first.

How am I so calm about this? WTF? They pulled out his freaking teeth! I'm seeing an RPG game in real life, dragons and goblins and vamps, oh my! But I'm still doing the job like this is all fucking normal. There's this thick ass blanket of fog between me and reality. A few deep breaths in through my nose out through my mouth stop the beginning stages of the impending panic attack, barely. What do they call this? The distancing of oneself from an event to cope with it? Searching my brain somewhat frantically for the right word, I startle when the loud buzz of the door finally being unlocked sounds.

Jesus H. Christ!

Dissociation, that's what it's called when you distance yourself from something so far that you're numb. Honestly, I'm not sure I'm ready to give up my dissociation yet. That means accepting reality which means allowing that I see things. There's a brush of air in front of my face and then something resembling a fairy—except with lots of teeth—brushes its tiny hand across my cheek and winks at me before flying away.

Well, that closes the debate because I'm not ready for whatever this reality is yet. Nope. For now. Damnit. Another deep breath and I push open the door with only a little bit of an issue with my shaking hands, manage to wiggle the cart through the door.

The scuffle of feet heralds my entrance followed closely by chairs scraping across the floor. I look around the edge of the cart at the guards who are standing with their hands on... swords? Why do they have swords? I blink several times in an attempt to clear away the vision. I even cover my freaky eye—they still have swords. Okay then not only is this place fucking odd, but they're also stuck in the 1700s.

"You're the new bait?" The tallest one asks.

Unsure how to answer that without saying something rude, I let the insult roll off of me and nod. Instead, I stare, I can't help it, he has an incredibly pointy chin. No joke at all, it comes to an actual point. The rest of his face is almost as angular, and the top of his head crowns into another sharp point. I have no idea what he's supposed to be, but he reminds of a villain from a comic book movie—that green one that liked to laugh a lot.

The annoying one.

"Don't turn your back on anyone. If you do and they get you, I'm not coming in to help you." With that said he sits back down, he and the others start laughing at something they're whispering about. I imagine whatever it is, concerns me and my predicted demise. Arrogant fuckers, the entire lot of the men I've met so far.

I do know a legitimate warning of danger when I hear one. Their glee about it doesn't hide the fact that it rings of truth. They genuinely believe something will happen to me in this place. Even though Vale said none would harm me.

Which part of the crazy is the right one?

Regardless, I still have a job to do. Looking at my list to get a good idea of the order of delivery, I give one glance down the rather dark hallway, with much thicker doors and a more prison-like feel to it. Well, there's nothing to be done about it. This is the last floor then I'll get to start once again on the first floor, cleaning and collecting trays. The duty list says I have to change any beds that need it, clean the floor and bathroom, as well as remove any garbage and dirty laundry. There's a cart specific for this in the laundry/cleaning room that I left downstairs. I've got to get through this first.

This floor has a different feel because there's this fog of tension that's saturating the air. Well, I guess not so different from that danger-Will-Robinson feeling that Vale gives me. I don't feel *in* any more danger than before, just that there is danger *here*. Which doesn't make any sense at all. Unless what he said actually holds water. Is it possible that he can predict or ensure that no one hurts me here? At least none of the patients. Well, I can't stand here like a ninny deciding what weird tract of thought to follow, they need their food, and I need to keep this job.

Unless the insanity of this entire mess awakens my common sense and I quit.

I stop at the first door, and the lack of a food tray slot instantly halts my momentum. How the hell am I supposed to get their food to them? The jingle of keys pulls my gaze up to the pointy-chinned guard, who's suddenly standing beside me. With a leer he hands me the ring of keys, each one marked with the number of what I'm assuming is a matching room.

"Most of them are restrained," he says and walks off.

I have to go into the room with them? I'm not sure how I feel about that because this is supposedly the most dangerous floor. Followed immediately by that thought is the question of why Vale isn't up here because old man or not he's dangerous. Which is then followed up by, why didn't I get a sword? Not that I have any idea how to use one. A nightstick maybe, I could wallop someone with that. Sword? Not so much. I'd probably end up lopping my body parts off with it instead of defending myself.

Sorting through the keys, I find the one that matches the room and with my stomach doing the mamba in apprehension, I open the door.

"Go away," a rough female voice says from inside the darkened room. I'm many things, but a coward isn't one of them, at least not most of the time. But something in that voice makes me hesitate for a split second.

"Hello to you too," I say, turning to grab her tray out of the bottomless cart and step into the room. It smells, there's no denying that. A quick look around in the dim light shows that there's no bathroom either. There's a bucket against the far wall, and there's only one purpose for a bucket in a situation like this. I imagine that's part of what I'm smelling. The rest, that's all bad hygiene. I also think that it's not the fault of the patient, either. The majority of the staff I've met here are tool bags, and I can absolutely see them ignoring the needs of the patients and quite possibly doing things to hurt them. Vale is an excellent example. I've never heard of a legit psychiatric hospital removing someone's teeth for biting. Muzzling them maybe, but never removing them. Although, I'm pretty sure I've read about atrocities being committed in the older ones that were that bad, or worse. You know, like the lobotomies.

I really need to do some major web searching when I get home. This is unacceptable.

"You're new." The lump on the bed says and with a whisper of moving cloth turns to look towards me. The only thing that keeps me from turning and running out of the room is the fact that I can clearly see the delicate shackles tying her to the bed.

The woman and that term is a loose one, has teeth like a raptor, eyes that are bright yellow and reptilian in nature.

Her hair, not that it's real hair—is feathers. Long, beautiful, green feathers with flashes of orange in their depths.

"You're one of the prettiest things I've ever seen," I blurt out. Her eyes widen in shock, and that toothy mouth of hers opens and then closes.

"What slop have they given me today?" she asks instead of saying whatever is dancing in her eyes. The tension in the room disappears as if it never were. The pressure inside of me relaxes as well. I feel like I passed some sort of test.

Given how there is a light of curiosity in her eyes now, maybe I did.

"Honestly, it looks like a raw duck, but I'm not completely up to date on my naked poultry," I answer, watching her face closely for any amusement. That's what I was going for and when she smiles—well, her version of smiling, I think—I smile in return. I hand her the tray and step back to give her room to eat without me being all up in her business.

"You are awfully calm, all things considered," she says, grabbing the leg of the duck and yanking it off with a cringe-worthy sound of flesh and bone tearing.

"Considered what?" I ask.

Watching her chew is morbidly fascinating, it genuinely looks like what I always imagined a T-Rex looked like taking a chunk out of a bronto.

Hey, I was a weird kid.

"I see the Blood Mark on your face," she comments, grabbing another hunk of meat. "Vale?" she asks, taking a large bite.

"Yes, he spit on me." Why am I being so honest? It's easier this way I reckon, nothing to be done about it now. I'm not much on lying if I can help it, one lie always turns into two and soon you're buried under the avalanche of them.

"I'm guessing you can see all manner of things now that you couldn't before?"

"Yes, hallucinations."

She chuckles, and I'm pretty sure pieces of chewed duck fall out of her mouth onto the filthy striped pajamas she's wearing.

"You're not hallucinating, something you'll realize soon enough," she says, pausing in her meal. "Are the guards being cordial to you?" Strange question to ask, but I shrug in response.

"I will be back through later and," I search for the words to use, opting to be blunt instead of delicate, "if you'd like to bathe I'll help you out with that." The duck drops onto the tray with a wet thud.

"You'd bathe me?" Why is that so shocking? It's a simple act, nothing dramatic.

Already committed, and not bothered by it, I say, "Yes, it's not meant to be insulting, but it smells like an outhouse in here."

The laughter this time is full on, she even slaps her thigh as she cackles—reminding me a bit of Athena in it. The smile that breaks free from me is unstoppable, and the last bit of tension in me relaxes. I know, really know, this woman won't hurt me.

"I'll see you when you come back around then, be mindful of the guards and if any of them hurt you... don't hesitate to let myself or Vale know."

"I can say the same. Do you mind telling me your name? All I have is your number, and that's a mouthful to say."

Another toothy smile, she says, "Gahna. And who might you be, almost human girl?"

I ignore the almost human bit, and reply, "Mel. I'll see you soon, Gahna." Turning, I go back to the door and with a heavy feeling of remorse relock it as I leave.

The dissection of the encounter starts immediately. Perhaps she killed someone and is only nice to them before she eats them? Na, I don't think she's the type to waste energy on it. Not the eating people part, because if I were her, I'd probably eat people, but that she befriends them before she eats them. I don't think it's random either. I have a feeling that there's always a reason. A good solid intuition. Although, I'm not sure if I can count on anything about this day being accurate at all.

I've completely flipped my damn lid. A fact that should make me run home like a little scared girl, makes me smile instead. Today is the most interesting day I think I've ever had in my life, and I kind of like it. I do imagine that when I get home, and the adrenaline and reality smack me in the fucking head—I'll think differently, but for now, I'll ride the more peaceful train of acceptance. I'll have to deal with the breakneck ride on the crazy train soon enough.

The next room's occupant remains unmoving on the bed, a small person quite possibly a child. Still, I say hello and set the tray on the end of the bed. Feeling like an intruder, I vow that I'll be a bit more assertive when I come back through. None of them have been bathed, or have had their rooms touched in God knows how long. I'm pretty sure that their shit buckets are mostly full and overflowing.

It's 2018, who uses buckets to shit in anymore unless they're camping? To me, that's the only time that anyone should be using a bucket, and even camping you could use a hole then cover it up with dirt. To me, that seems preferable to a stinky pail. Why these folks don't have standard bathrooms is another mystery. There must be all kinds of laws being broken withholding things like that.

Vale's teeth, iron shackles, weird food and now, no bathrooms. How is this place still open?

Then, of course, my brain goes to the spooky shit. The walking skeletons, the nail painting dragons, and super cute fairies that wink at me. Why is it that part of me hopes that some of this is real? Walking, talking fantasies from child-hood. Except these are all prisoners in some demented shit hole that pulls out their teeth.

Fuck me.

Swallowing the rant I want to have, I continue. Each room I open, to whatever monster or creature my imagination concocts, I greet with a smile. I somehow manage to keep from feeling sorry for them and let them have their pride, but provide the same as I offered Gahna. Something I think is a simple kindness and a necessary one. There are ones in worse conditions than she was, some I'm not even sure can move. Most look hungry; some also look defeated. By the time I get to the last room, my heart is so heavy that I'm having trouble looking at the guards without hitting one of them with a tray.

There's no doubt in my mind that I'm reporting this place. I'm not sure how I'll do it, but it's totally happening. No one should live this way when they're ill. Vale was so right. This place is not safe or supportive.

Turning the key in the rusty lock, I fight to unlatch it and finally break down into bracing one foot against the door when I pull. Eventually it gives, and after I windmill a few times to keep from landing on my ass, I open the door. The fetid smell stops me dead in my tracks. There's something different in this room.

"Why do you greet us?" The voice is faint, but I manage to hear it. My eyes seek out the speaker, lying on a bare mattress, no blankets, no comfort at all. This time there are four shackles; the usual two restraining its hands, and two more binding its feet. Bent at an odd angle, he's got his hands tucked between his knees, and those knees pulled up to his waist. On his bare back are large open welts that I bet are the thickness of my middle finger.

WTF?

"No answer?" He prompts.

Clearing my throat, I say, "Because you all deserve at least that much."

"Even if we are insane prisoners that they portray us as?"

"Even more so then."

The man chuckles and turns his head slightly to look at me over his shoulder. My mouth falls open in shock. It's like looking at a younger Vale, just like the one I saw when we had that moment. His hair moves when he turns back away from me, the absence of those white eyes making breathing a bit easier again. His hair is solid white and long, matted and filthy. Have any of them been bathed at all in the last month? Year?

I make the same offer to him that I made to the others.

"Yes," he says, and I sense our brief, confusing conversation is over. I set his tray down behind him; this one is a covered dish, its contents a mystery. I have this awful feeling that whatever is under that dish's cover will freak me the fuck out.

Backing out of the room I relock the door and head back towards the elevator. It's time for me to have a brief break and I'm finding that it's one I need to take. This emotional wringer has me flat out exhausted. I have no idea how people willingly put themselves in situations to face things like this. I'm torn between sneaking in the bathroom to have a good cry or releasing all the patients and burning this place down.

I opt for the bathroom—this time.

CHAPTER EIGHT

In order to see birds it is necessary to become part of the silence.
~*Robert Lynd*

GIVING out the trays took almost two hours. It's incredible how fast that time went. My break is a half-hour, and for fifteen minutes I hide in the sickly orange bathroom. By the time I crawl out of the horror bathroom from the sixties, my stomach decides to wake up. On wooden feet, I clomp back to the employee lounge in search of my leftovers. Stopping short outside of the door, I look up into the gentle face of Connie. Without a word, she hands me a paper bag and gives me a quick pat on my arm. On the other side of the door behind her, I can hear the voices of some of the guards, not people I want to talk to right now.

"You could go eat in the main room, no one is ever there,"

Connie says walking off towards the kitchen. My esteem for her grows. She knew I didn't want to go in there with the rest of them to be belittled or harassed. They are the ones who hurt the people here.

They are the ones who need to pay for it.

Somehow, I must find a way to help, although I'm not entirely sure if anything I do will. How it's continued for this long I don't understand. I can't be the only one to have felt this way. People came before me, and I don't believe Vale's boast of killing them. A murderer wouldn't be on the first floor or have the freedoms they do compared to what I saw on the third. That means that there had to be others who saw this and tried to do something. Right? Anyone with a drop of humanity left in them wouldn't leave these poor people like this. I pull my phone out of my pocket to discover I still have no service. There goes googling on my break.

Chewing on my bottom lip, I give a distracted smile of greeting to the small green blob that stops and waves at me from the floor. I wave back and walk around him. Unless something has done awful things, they all deserve respect and compassion, even blobs.

Finding the main room as empty as it was before, completely unchanged too, I settle myself at the table farthest away from the nurse's mausoleum. Opening up the bag I find a thick bacon sandwich, a small bag of sliced apples, and a cold diet soda. It's like Connie speaks directly to my stomach's soul. Something heavy enough to be filling but light enough to not weigh me down for the rest of my shift. Biting into one triangle shaped half, I chew with relish and find myself feeling lighter of spirit.

I will find a way to help these people.

My eyes immediately land on the girl walking towards me. For the most part, she looks normal compared to what I've been seeing, but not entirely. Her eyes are a bright, solid white. Incredibly vivid in her dirty face. The floor-length nightgown she's wearing is even nastier, hiding all but her filthy blood encrusted bare toes peeking out at the dirty hem. Swallowing the lump in my throat, I attempt to smile.

"Would you like half a sandwich? It's bacon," I ask, pushing the other half of the sandwich across the table. "There are some apples too."

Watching me with caution, she slowly works her way to the table and pulls the chair out. Her head bobs as her freaky eyes flick between me and the sandwich that I can hear her stomach growling for. She sits and with a final, longer look at me grabs the offered food and crams the entire half in her mouth. While she chews, her cheeks puff out like this adorable little chipmunk A malnourished chipmunk, who has white eyes and from what I saw, a mouthful of sharp teeth.

"I'm not blind," she says through the gob of chewed bread and meat.

"I didn't think you were." Which is nothing but the truth, strangely enough.

"Most do," she says swallowing. I imagine the bread has made her thirsty, so in response to that I open a can of soda and slide it over to her. With both hands, she grabs it and gulps it greedily. When she sits the mostly empty can back down her eyes are watering as that gaze fixes on me once again.

"I thought you needed to be looked after. I don't remember you from mealtime." Now that I think about it, I can't recall seeing her at all.

"I'm normally on the third floor. I decided to take a walk today."

The urge to ask her how she got through the doors and past the guard opens my mouth, but I immediately change my mind and say instead, "That's lovely. Would you like a bath today too?" Her head tilts to the side, and she smiles. Yep, lots of sharp teeth. In and out of technicolor land.

"That would be something I have not had the pleasure of in a long time." She wipes her mouth with the back of her hand. "As scary as this all is, accept it, and don't call the authorities. They have no power here, and it will only put you in danger."

The shock of her statement makes me drop the bag of apples out of my hand. I decide to leave them for the moment and ask, neutrally, "Which room is yours?"

"I'm not sure, but you'll find me when you need to," she says rising to her feet. "Thank you for the sandwich. Where I come from, sharing food is a sign of high respect," she pauses then continues, "Especially, when it's all they have." Turning she walks away, and I swear to god she disappears before she turns the corner.

As I eat the apples, I contemplate the place where she disappeared. Why did she tell me not to call the authorities? Hell, how did she know I was thinking about it? No, not thinking, planning on it. Now what the hell do I do? Any instinct I have that's worth a shit is saying to listen to her, but how these people are being treated needs to stop.

I'm incredibly confused, and my inner moral compass is having spasms.

Finishing up my lunch, I toss my garbage in the trash and head back to the employee lounge. I need caffeine, and since I gave her my soda, I need something else. I need it so much that I'm willing to brave the soup they call coffee in the lounge. As I walk past the kitchen, the silver tray cart is pushed out and on top of it, almost shining like a beacon, is another cold soda. Connie is my hero today, hell, maybe even the month. Or year. Probably the year.

Laughing, I yell a thank you and start pushing the monstrosity of a cart towards the laundry room. Grabbing the smaller laundry cart, I decide how to go about this. If I go through first to get the trays, then I'll have to take even more time to come here and get this cart to do everything else. Or, I can merely take both carts and do everything I need at once. Thankfully, since the laundry cart is smaller, I can tug it behind me with one hand and push the meal cart with the other. The progress is slow, and I bump into things now and then, but this is part of my tasks for the night, in addition to meals—clean rooms, clean patients. I still have to give out more trays, and the clock is ticking, but I'm determined to be finished before I leave at 4 a.m.

Well, I won't know until I give it a try.

Checking the new list on the side of the cart, I see that Vale is now first. Not that I genuinely mind, no matter how much I protest. He's been on my mind since I met him hours ago, way more than I want him to be. And the other guy, the one with the scars. I have no name for him, but there's something that feels somewhat the same about him and Vale.

I volunteered to bathe him too. What the hell is wrong with me?

Oh, I know, I've lost my fucking mind.

VALE GREETS me pleasantly from the doorway, he's casually leaning against. "Good day, Mel." From the doorway, he's casually leaning against. I do my best to ignore the jump in my pulse and the fact that he looks... brighter. I swear it's like someone turned up his wattage.

"Hello there! I'm going to give your room a quick clean while you eat—drink, your... drink." Wow, I'm lame as shit.

Almost like he can hear my inner monologue, he watches me with amusement. A smile tilts the edges of his lips as his eyes lighten like tiny light bulbs. They've got such a look of knowing in them that I feel that he can see into every shadow of my soul, like he knows me at the deepest level. Distractedly, I reach inside the cart and yank my hand back when something stings my finger. Looking at it, I watch as a single ruby red drop pearls on the tip of my finger.

An idea pops into my mind, a crazy idea and I choose to act on it before I can think about it. The tray holding his shake is right in front of me and for some fucked up reason I hold my finger over it, letting the blood drop into it. I even take it further by squeezing another few drops into it. I mean, he did say he needs human blood, and it's already pig's blood, so I'm not exactly grossing it up. I don't have any weird diseases, I—fuck it.

Grabbing the tray before I decide to toss it in the garbage can on the end of the laundry cart, I hold it out to him. With that deep look, he gingerly plucks the cup off the tray, as it gets closer to his face, I watch the disgust fade and his eyes brighten as he tilts it up downing it in one long swallow. I stand there like a mute dumbass and watch the muscles in his throat work, wondering what it'd be like to touch him there. If the skin is as soft as it looks, if it… holy fuck. The wrinkly skin of his neck starts to tighten visibly and when he looks at me again his face—his face is at least fifteen years younger.

I lean one hand on the doorframe to steady myself from the sudden onset of dizziness.

What the fuck?

"You've been upstairs?" he asks in that same tone of ease.

I try to talk only to find my mouth too dry to form words. Sucking on my tongue to get some saliva in there I clear my throat and try again. "Yes."

Needing to do something other than gape at the old man who isn't old anymore, I walk around him and start stripping his neatly made bed. There's a thin layer of dust on the threadbare cover which makes me wonder if he ever uses it.

"Are you at all curious why they restrain them?" I am, but I don't say that.

Instead, I say, "Why do I feel like you should be on the third floor with them?"

He chuckles and says, "They think they have tamed me."

Balling up the dirty blanket and sheets, I set them on the floor while I put on new ones, whether he sleeps on there or not he needs a clean one. It gives me something to do other than asking the million questions I have. I know they haven't tamed him if nothing else about today is true, that is. Carefully coiled violence lay just under his skin. His younger skin. I try to avoid looking at him but fall in the trap despite myself.

He looks my age now, probably even younger. His hair is long and as white as his eyes, his face is—Christ, his face is beautiful. "No one should be as pretty as you are, Vale," I mumble and head into the bathroom which is used, thankfully. At least I know he pees like everyone else. Going back to the cart with a basket full of dirty towels, I dump them in the bin and grab clean toiletries and cleaning supplies.

A quick scrub later I come back out into the room to find Vale blocking my way. Using my wrist to move loose hair out of my sweaty face, I frown at him.

"You can almost see the truth of this place now, can't you?" he says smiling. I drop the bottle of cleaner. All his teeth are back—long, sharp and as white as his hair. I can see this fact with both eyes.

"The truth? Well, Vale, the truth is I probably belong here with you and might end up that way before it's all said and done."

"I can't allow that. They would break you in here," he says stepping closer to me, his smile dimming. "What if I told you that this place is a prison for creatures like you and me?"

"I'm calling the authorities when I leave here." His fingertips lightly touch my elbow, he leaves them there while he bends down and picks up the cleaner which he hands to me.

"No, that will do nothing more than put you in danger." I feel his frustration, unexpected as it is. "Soon you will understand everything, Melantha. I'd explain it all right now, but I don't think you'd believe it, and the game of denial you'd play would take too long." His thumb strokes my skin before he pulls away, reluctantly. "There's a reason you're here, and these fools have no idea what they have let loose in their zoo."

I hear his words, I do, but my brain is foggy and not ready to deal with them.

"My blood made you younger," I say in a rush.

He nods his head but remains silent.

"How much more will fix you completely?" Those eyes light up, and he leans his face down to the level of mine. Knowing exactly what I'm asking even with me trying to find a diplomatic way of saying blood.

"A few drops of yours every day or ten full-grown men." I almost laugh until I see he's being completely earnest.

"I've flipped my lid, haven't I?" I blurt out.

"Oh, not in the least. You'll see that soon enough. I'd say rather sooner than you'd like." Quick as a snake he kisses the corner of my mouth and then withdraws to sit on the edge of his bed, making a face as it squeaks from his weight.

I think that it was meant to be a more graceful exit from the conversation. A laugh creeps out of me, and I'm still laughing when I finish the next two rooms. On the third I'm doing everything I can to keep from crying. I don't want to be crazy.

Out in the hallway after the last room, I'm staring at the ground contemplating leaving early with some made up illness when I walk right into a warm body. Strong hands straighten me up, and I look up into the bright eyes of Vale.

"I realize that I no longer have the social skills I once had. You are not safe in your ignorance. Come back to me before you leave for the day, I'll explain things the right way." Once again, he releases me with that odd reluctance and turns to go back to his room. For several seconds I stand there staring at his doorway before I give a long sigh.

Every room I clean, every miserable person I see, makes me question my doubt about everything. It makes me think that maybe, just maybe, I'm not losing my mind, that perhaps I'm seeing something new and different for the first time in my black and white life. Maybe. Or maybe I'm so far gone that I'm laying drugged up on a hard bed in some random hallway with flickering lights and orderlies eating their lunches while laughing at the delirious woman babbling about vampires and dragons.

Leaning against the wall of the elevator that I finally managed to get everything into, I let my shoulders droop as my poor mind tries to fix the fracture that's getting wider by the minute. I've always trusted my instincts, even when they went against logic. They never steer me wrong. It's when I don't listen to them that I end up in trouble or almost married to a guy who still gives his mom foot massages in the bathtub.

Right now, those instincts are telling me this is all real. That this place, these people in it, this weird shit I'm seeing is *all* real. While my logic, as fickle as it usually is, says it's absolutely impossible. Dragons and zombies and fairies and beautiful white-haired vampires can't exist. Don't exist. Human beings don't believe in such things. But I can hear them, see them, smell them. My fingers trace over the still tingly corner of my mouth. Feel them, I can feel them.

Can a hallucination be that vivid?

The doors open, and I struggle to get both carts out of the elevator, without any assistance from the guards who ignore my presence. Assholes. I'm having a mental crisis, and one of them is looking at Playboy.

"I'm surprised you're still alive. I'm betting you're dead by the end of the week." The fatter one of the two says, his face is unfamiliar. How often do they switch guards here?

Ignoring him I move on and discover now that I have a rhythm I can move more quickly. As before, some speak to me but most don't, and this time I have to go into their rooms. The keys are thrown at me; I barely catch them before they plow into my face. "Thanks, asshole," I mutter.

These rooms are not as well kept as the first floor, but at least they have bathrooms. I offer the same things as before. I end up helping a few bathe and all of them into clean clothes. I change all their disgusting bed sheets. I swear I don't think anyone has cared for them in months. Maybe longer. With some elbow grease, I even manage to scrub their bathrooms to some semblance of clean.

Most of them don't talk, but some do. I learn some of their names and not a single one tries to hurt me. They don't like the guards though, not one bit. When I was bathing Samson, a lovely little leprechaun—seriously, his skin is even green, and he's sad because they took his gold coin—stopped by to say hello. During that time, he sat on Samson's bed, his short legs swinging as he told me his entire life story. I plan on getting his coin back the first chance I have. It's sitting on the desk with a few other belongings from the people I'm caring for. One in particular is a dirty teddy bear that's seen better days, but Lila's Mom gave it to her before the magic hunters killed her. All because she's a pixie.

At this point, I'm not second-guessing any of these things anymore. It takes too much energy. I'll break down later. They need me to have it together as much as possible. It's not like anyone else gives a fuck about them.

The second floor is done much more quickly than I

expected. I leave them with their dinners and clean rooms and head up to the third floor. Coming off the elevator, I slam into the floor before I even have time to look around. Above me, laughter beats down on me.

Climbing to my feet, I look down at my poor knee. The uniform is intact, but I can feel the sting beneath the rough fabric. There'll be a hell of a bruise tomorrow, and it's possible that there's a bit of blood. Brett, the dickhead guard from earlier, pokes me with his finger, pushing me a little and laughs harder.

"Aww is the new girl gonna cry?" Who the hell talks that way?

"Are you fucking ten?" I demand, relaxing my stance in preparation to break his fucking fingers.

"Brett, get over here. She'll be gone soon enough. You can laugh then." The pointy chinned one calls.

"I thought you didn't like the third floor, Brett?" I ask him, pleased to see his face pale.

"He has to work it just like the rest of us, the pussy." Pointy chin teases. Brett's face turns red, and he glares at me.

For a moment he contemplates hitting me, I can see it clearly on his face. Something stops him, luckily for him. I really will break his fingers. Maybe he realizes I'll make good on my threat or perhaps he decides to use his brain, either way, he goes back to the door and shuts it leaving me out in the hallway. I push the button and wait. I might break his fingers, anyway.

The door buzzes, and when it opens, I wheel the cart in. Brett laughs from the desk, choosing to take the higher road, for now, I start opening doors. This floor is going to take me the longest. I grit my teeth at the condition of the first patient. He's probably thirteen or fourteen at best and is covered in sores and filth. I don't miss the stripes of a belt either.

"You ready for that bath now?" Studying me a moment out of moss green eyes he then smiles and exposes the only two pointy teeth in his head. Reminds me of a snake, in a cool way. I go out to the laundry cart and open the side door. Connie told me anything I'll need would be in it, so I dig around inside until I feel the metal of a small hip bath. Pulling it out I look back inside the cart's dark emptiness. I shut the door, open it and look again.

How the hell does that work?

I dig around for the shampoo and soap I'll need. When my hands find what I'm looking for, I decide not to question it. I grab a stack of towels then head back into the room.

"What's your name?" I ask sitting the tub down.

"Min," he answers in a voice that doesn't match the youth of him.

Shit, I need water. Well, I'll try the magic cart again. Ha, magic cart. Opening it up I pull out the bucket I need and turn to the taps that are on the wall between every room.

Honestly, I can't say I remember them being there before. It's not the strangest thing I've experienced today, so I roll with it. After a few sputters, the rusted faucet awards me hot water. Five buckets full of water later, the bathtub is full, plus I have enough to rinse with. I turn my back to him, so Min can undress and get inside the tub.

Nudity doesn't faze me, I've worked with infirm people before—it's a bath, not a date. He smiles at me when I turn to him with soap in hand. He's still grinning a few minutes later after he's scrubbed his skin hard enough to make it pink. After we wash his hair, I pull a stool over and start combing through the matted strands.

"You're not like the others. You're like us," he says, still smiling. His eyes are closed, and his head is resting on my knees.

"That's what I keep hearing," I tease. "If I hurt you I'm

sorry ahead of time, your hair is a bit fu—fudged," I catch the cuss worse at the last minute.

"This is a great kindness."

"Na, it's a bath. Kindness is me attempting to cut those dagger toenails of yours. That we'll save for tomorrow." He giggles at my words.

"Who injured your knee?" The smile has faded off his face, and his green eyes are on me. Finishing up with his hair I pat his peach-fuzz covered cheek and tilt his head up, so I can stand. At this stage in my day, I don't even ask how he knows about my knee.

"One of the fairy fuckers," slips out. His full-bellied laugh makes me chuckle with him.

"He's not a fairy, but they think their little butterfly wings makes them special." I turn so he can stand and wrap a towel around himself, giving him as much privacy as I can. He's like the millionth person I've helped get clean today.

"So, what are they?"

"They were mostly human once upon a time. Their otherness was a payment for service, they're not born like us." That's another person hinting that I'm more than human. What the hell do I do with that?

"They're dicks," I add.

"Truer words have never been spoken."

I dash out to the cart and get him clean clothes, including the hospital socks. The cart provides all I request. I could get used to this. He's dressed and clean and is now eating his food on his changed bed. I straighten up the room as best as I can, including tossing the shit bucket down the garbage chute. Snooping around in his space I find a door, that's locked of course, and after a million tries I find a key that fits it. When I open the creaky door, I discover a bathroom. Dusty, unused but intact and when I turn the faucet, water comes out with no issues—the toilet still flushes.

Now, what the hell is this?

Min is standing when I come out of the room that I leave unlocked. I put my finger to my lips and, "Shhh."

He mirrors my movement, and I wave to him as I grab his discarded dishes and move onto the next room. We won't tell the guards that I left his room unlocked too. I did the same thing on the second floor with no regrets.

The frail old man turns from his spot on the floor when I enter.

"Are you an angel?" he asks in a raspy voice.

Fighting tears, I go through the process I went through with Min, except I help him shave the beard off his face. I find a bathroom in his room too, which I leave unlocked.

Every room in this place makes me hate the people who run it a little more each time. Until I get to the final room. Vale's almost twin. Now that I've seen a younger version of Vale I can get away with saying that. They look so alike it's freaky. I wonder if they're brothers? I should ask.

As I walk into the room, he doesn't turn to greet me this time, and I immediately see why. Blood is pooled thick around him and in little offshoots trailing towards the door. I quickly grab a bunch of towels and run to him, carefully I move him enough to check for a pulse and find a weak one, but it's still there. I need to get their doctor. I'm not an idiot, I know he's dying. Losing all that blood would kill anyone.

"No. I'll heal." His words stop me dead in my tracks.

"Jesus, you're bleeding everywhere. This is more than I can fix."

"You sound as if you care." The cynicism in his voice is thick.

"Of course, I care, I'm here still, aren't I?" His quiet chuckle turns into a wet cough. "Who did this to you?" I ask quietly, gently pushing against the wounds on his chest with the towel that becomes immediately saturated with blood.

Panic is teasing me. I'm so out of my fucking depth here. What if he dies?

"I'll heal once I feed." I blink at him stupidly for a minute. Will food fix this? Jumping up I jog to the cart and reach in for his tray. It's heavier than the last one, still covered from view and I hurry it back to him. Supporting his back, I help him sit up enough to eat and step back. "You'll want to look away," he says, his hand resting on the handle at the top of the dish cover.

"Okay," I say and turn. I have no idea what's on that plate, but if it makes him better, I don't care. All I know is that he thinks it'll freak me out and he's probably right. The sounds I'm hearing behind me don't help. Growling, crunching... gross chewing noises. It's worse than hearing Gahna eat.

"You know, I don't know your name," I hint. The sounds are getting a bit disgusting and I figure talking will cover some of it up.

"Tavin," he answers around a mouthful of whatever he's eating. Tavin? I figured since they're twins the names would match a bit more. Maybe they're not brothers? "We are brothers... of a sort."

"Did you just read my fucking mind?" I demand, catching myself right as I'm about to turn around. Vale drinks blood, and if Tavin is his brother—of a sort, whatever that means— then I imagine he's chewing something that's like blood is for Vale. Something I don't want to see.

Maybe those bodies on the hooks weren't so far-fetched after all?

"No, it was the obvious question since you met him first." At least he doesn't sound like he's talking around a mouthful of crunchy dicks anymore.

"Feeling better?" I ask, strained.

"You can turn now." I do and almost turned right back around. His face is a bloody mess but not from injuries because there isn't a mark on his face. It's from whatever he was eating. Yep, don't want to know what he was chomping on. I grab the tray and practically throw it into the open doors of the cart.

Bodies. Hooks. Me vomiting. Not something I want to do or think about right now.

"Do you feel like getting cleaned up?" I ask, instead of tossing my partially digested apples on the floor. Stepping back into the room armed with what I'll need for him to bathe, I force my thoughts to move onto the next task. I can have nightmares about his lunch later. I no longer need the bathtub because I discovered earlier that they all have bathrooms, but they were denied them. I search out the door and unlock it.

Well, I plan on changing that. If they really don't want me to call people to come in to help them, I won't. God, I can't believe I'm accepting that, but it is what it is, and that's the end of it. *But* I can, however, give them the simple pleasure of a real fucking toilet and shower. They'll not sit filthy and hungry around me anymore.

"Being clean is not a pleasure I've had in a very long time," he says climbing to his feet. Without waiting, I go into the bathroom and turn on the single light. It flickers, and after a few blinks a light buzz fills the air, and it remains on. The room is tidy, just unused and dusty.

Hurriedly I clean some of the surfaces he'll be touching and put a towel on the floor in front of the shower. I turn and almost run into him, watching me from the doorway. Instead of saying anything that my brain is juggling around I shove the towels at him, then squeeze past him, doing everything I can to touch his body as minimally as possible.

Yes, I'm that weird.

"He'll be waiting for you to return to him," his words freeze me in my tracks, "Don't keep him waiting, he gets cranky." With that said to my tense back the water turns on, and I hear him moving the curtain around.

"I need to help you finish," I mumble defiantly.

"I'm not a child, Mel." It's an absolute dismissal, and I'll look like an idiot if I stand there arguing with him about it.

Sighing, I trudge outside my feet essentially dragging on the floor. The dread in my stomach is telling me the next conversation I have with Vale will change my life irrevocably. Delaying it won't change it, but damnit, I do what I want. Mostly.

When did I accept that this shit might be real?

After a moment, I realize precisely when. While I was helping Min, he looked so happy with something as simple as getting his hair combed, when he fought the automatic flinch from me cleaning the damage to his too thin body, when he looked at me like I was his hero, if only for those few quiet moments in his turbulent life.

In fact, I realize in my turbulent, lonely life that for the first time in years I haven't felt lonely all day long—not one single time. There's so much to do here, so much to change here. So many who need help. Help that, for once, I can give. Even if it's something as simple as a good meal and a spot of deodorant. Or a simple tube of toothpaste, which I've passed out freely today.

At least until the people who own this place find out what I'm doing and fire me because I'm entirely sure that will happen. As optimistic as I'd like to be about things, they will fire me. I always get let go, from every single job I've ever had. Yet, this is the first one I've ever cared about. It's been six hours, and it feels like a lifetime. This place is full of suffering and pain; no matter how monstrous my insane mind makes some of them appear, I care, and I hurt for them.

My Mom has always told me I'm too soft sometimes, in this instance she's probably right.

CHAPTER NINE

The sound of birds stops the noise in my mind.
~Carly Simon

AFTER I RETURN THE CARTS, in preparation for the next meal, I head towards Vale's room. Accomplishment is a warm feeling in my chest after I managed to get all of my duties completed—except for the last meal. Smiling a little bit, I whistle as I walk, feeling like I'm on top of the world. Holy hell that was a lot of shit to do, but it felt good to be busy. It felt good to be useful. I'm in such a good mood, in fact, that I even smile and wave at the guards on the first floor as I breeze past them on my way to Vale's room.

As expected, I get a few dirty looks and then I'm pointedly ignored.

I've forgotten what it's like to be in a truly good mood. Most of my life has gone to shit and remained there for so long that I didn't remember how nice *this* feels. I've spent the majority of the last ten years feeling sorry for myself and depressed because nothing ever seemed to work out right. Especially—my thoughts screech to a halt.

Vale's sitting on his bed with his head in his hands, well, what's left of his bed. The mattress is mostly in pieces, and the frame is tossed against the far wall, the metal twisted and bent. His long white hair is stained red, and I can see blood dried on his arms and bare back. The rest of his meager possessions are irreversibly destroyed, among them his few books are gutted with their pages strewn about the floor like corpses from a battle.

I don't miss the wet blood all over the place, either.

"Vale?" I ask in concern pausing a few steps from him. Approaching an injured animal isn't something you rush into, not unless you want to get bit. Vale is putting off that dangerous aura, and the anger bleeding from him is so cold that goosebumps raise on my skin.

Cold anger is some scary shit.

"Have you finished already?" he asks, standing. The shine of his teeth as he grimaces from pain, brings me completely to his side. Hesitantly, touching his elbow, I get a good look at some of his wounds. With a frown of worry, I dash out into the hallway to get the chair that I saw sitting out there against the wall. Bringing it in, I set it beside him and steer him gently but determinedly towards it. Without apology, I push him into the seat. With a look of exasperation directed at me, he sinks into the seat and sighs as he settles.

"What happened?"

"The guards and I had a small disagreement," he says, breathing shallowly enough I notice. The bruises marring his sides concern me. I bet his ribs are broken.

"How bad of shape are they in?" Going into the bathroom, I wet a few washcloths in cold water and come back out.

"They are... unharmed." The last word is essentially spat out. He's not happy about this fact.

"Why?" Honestly, I'm not super happy about it either.

"They cannot know that I am stronger," he whispers just loud enough for me to hear him.

Kneeling, I set to work cleaning him up, completely ignoring his protests. They're not serious ones anyhow. They beat the shit out of him, hard-core, and he needs the help I can give him.

The damage to his person pisses me right off.

"Do you like music?" I ask to distract him and maybe myself from what happened to him and from the pain I'm inflicting trying to clean the wounds I can see on his arms.

"Mmm. It's been a few years since I've heard any," he answers in a tight voice, his jaw clenched. He's in a lot of pain. I can feel it in the way his muscles quiver when I touch him. The reaction is slight, something I'd miss if I weren't somehow wound up with him.

"God, don't tell me you only like listening to classical music—while sniffing fancy crystal glasses filled with red wines that are fourteen million years old and made from digested grapes of some weird monkey-troll." It's what popped into my head and came directly out of my mouth.

For a solid two-seconds, he looks at me with sparkling eyes before throwing his head back and laughing. Even as he squeezes his side with one hand, he keeps chuckling. Well, at least my stupid humor is good for something.

"I thought vampires had magical healing powers or some shit?" I ask.

His face sobers, and he shocks me when he leans forward and rests his forehead against mine. Our eyes are inches apart, and I can feel his breath on my lips. He looks... tired and I don't like this look on him.

"They can't see that I'm becoming whole again, I need the energy to maintain that secret, so I can't use it to heal."

"What will make the pain better? Ice?" *He's a vampire, Mel, why the hell would ice help?*

"Only what you have already gifted me with can fix this problem, beautiful. A lot of it."

"How much is a lot?" I whisper.

He chuckles and says, "Do you know what you ask?" I do, yes. I'm asking him if my blood will help him because I'm falling for this fantasy world.

"Take what you need to chase the pain away."

The whites of his eyes overtake the pupils, and I sense the change within him, around him. The hair on my arms is standing straight up from it.

"Do not run," he warns before grabbing my face with both hands.

Cool lips cover mine, the pressure incredibly gentle—at first. His lips remain still and let me adjust to their presence. Our eyes are open, locked into a place of no going back. The sharp sting from one of his teeth as it lightly grazes my bottom lip is the only warning I get before I feel a lot more of them sink into my lip.

It hurts a lot, and a moan of pain slips through our joined mouths. My first instinct is to pull away from him then to run as fast and as far as I can from this place and never come back. Thankfully, that panicky feeling fades as quickly as it happens. The sharp pain becomes a dull throb as he loosens his teeth's grip on me. A warm, soft tongue swirls around those sharp teeth that are now only shallowly sunk into my skin and leaves a line of heat in its path as it dips into my mouth. On instinct, my tongue meets his. They tangle together stroking each other softly and retreating only to return, leaving the taste of copper and Vale in its place. The hold on my face softens as he sucks my lip into his mouth.

The pull is completely and utterly the most erotic experience of my life.

Fingers root their way into my hair, pulling me even closer to the mouth that's no longer biting and is now simply devouring mine. And the entire time his eyes hold mine. He releases me, slowly, a bit of flesh at a time. I watch the wounds on his face pull his blood back into his body and seal closed. I watch the thirty-something looking face, become even more youthful, more ethereal. The long hair that's grazing my arms grows more lustrous and thicker.

The mother fucker is the poster boy for hair products all over the world at this point. However, pretty or not, his face can never be mistaken for anything but male—defined, strong jaw, strong roman nose, and winged eyebrows—that give his eyes an even more inhuman look to them. He also has a widow's peak, a perfect one that makes me want to run a fingertip over the small point of it.

"Well, that was different," I say and laugh nervously, sitting back on my heels. I'm not even sure how I got on my knees. "Don't you need more than that?" That's about as coherent as I can talk right now because now I can honestly say I know what it's like to be kissed completely senseless.

"To be at full strength, yes. You flatter me with your gift, but I'm afraid that you do not possess enough blood in your little body to sate my hunger... at least, that hunger." He smiles, and one sharp tooth winks at me.

Did Vale just flirt with me? His smile widens, and the predatory look he's currently giving me is all male. *Horny* male. Well, shit.

"You are rather accepting about our monstrous... appetites," he comments, running a finger down my cheek with affection. I shiver, and he smiles again—goddamn hormones and pretty vampires.

"Lions eat baby gazelles because they need meat not

because they're evil monsters. I reckon that's no different from you needing blood to survive. Which I might add is cleaner than Tavin's eating habits. He gets the schmutz all over his face." I wave my hand in front of my face to emphasize.

I'm also fully aware I'm nervous chattering.

"What do you think of Tavin?" he asks mildly. Sensing a trap, I shrug. The look on his face isn't jealousy; it's too intense for that. If anything, I'd say it's speculative with a dash of amusement.

"You two are brothers," I blurt out. This time he shrugs, completely avoiding my blatant hint for more information. In my opinion, they're more than likely identical twins because standing side by side most people would have a hard time telling them apart. Same sharp white eyes, same white hair, same widow's peak. Even their teeth are identical.

The difference that I can see is in the way they hold themselves. I'll pay more attention in the future to see if I can spot any other differences, it will be like putting a puzzle together. I like puzzles. For now, I'll let it drop. I don't think I know the right questions to ask yet, asking the wrong ones is a waste of time for both of us.

Frowning at my own hypocrisy, I ask the next question that pops into my head, "Does it always have to be people?" Vale nods. "Okay, how about just bad people? I can handle bad people being eaten or drank, or whatever pre-digestive process happens."

"Define bad people, Mel?" Is he really asking me to give him specifics on who I feel is acceptable for him to eat?

Rolling with it I say, "Child predators are top of the list."

"You feel very strongly about this particular type of 'bad' person," he muses.

Needing to be busy I climb to my feet and start picking up what I can in his room. "When I was six years old, my best

—only friend, Neva, and I were as thick as thieves. We did everything together back then," I smile sadly at the memories of two little girls finding each other in this shitty world. I continue, "She was probably the closest thing I ever had to a sibling, but one Friday she wasn't at the bus stop. We had a sleepover planned that night. So I got worried that maybe she was sick," I swallow the lump in my throat. Some things never stop aching. "After school, I went to her house to check up on her because cell phones weren't a thing, and there were cops everywhere," the breath I take is shaky but doesn't stop me from continuing. "Neva was kidnapped right out of her bed the night before."

"Did they find her?" he asks softly.

"A week later her body was found in a parking lot stuffed in one of those half-sized suitcases that people try to trick the airlines with." Clearing my throat, I continue the avalanche of fuckery. "She was brutalized and then strangled. The men who did it, the mother—" I swallow the tears that threaten. "The men claimed that strangling her was in the heat of the moment and a pure accident. They pled guilty to rape of a minor... and manslaughter. They were out on good behavior fifteen years later." Gritting my teeth, I work through the blush of the rage that once nearly consumed me. "One of them, Rick, kidnapped another girl and murdered her his first week out. He was sent back to prison where he should've remained to begin with. The other one, Stan, he's supposedly seeking treatment and not offending." I scoff, there's no cure for pedophilia. There's no cure for a child murderer of any kind, at least, not one that keeps them walking this earth.

"The justice system is so fucking broken that it let him walk free after something that awful. I mean, if he'd been caught with some weed or cocaine he'd have done thirty years. But rape a little girl and murder her and you walk in fifteen." I take a calming breath and shove my anger back down. "If someone can do something useful and painful with that worthless piece of shit, that's good in my book." And it is. I'll slather him with BBQ sauce myself. "Predators like that are much more of a monster than one who eats people like him."

Vale crosses the room and takes the broken piece of ceramic that I'm gripping tightly enough to cut into my palm. I didn't even realize I was doing it. Lifting my palm to his mouth, he licks it like a tall, good-looking, man-cat. That touch evaporates all those old emotions, and I discover that I'm almost smiling.

"Bad people only?" he asks. Going along with everything I nod. He could probably ask me to run naked through the hall right now, and I'd agree. I'm a captive in this moment between us, and he knows it. "Done." The word echoes in the room and I feel the reverberation in my soul.

WTF?

Needing to get away from the intensity of being close to him I pull my hand from his and head towards the door, making myself walk fast instead of running like the panic fluttering around in my chest is demanding I do.

"Have to get meals out again," I mutter, dodging around the corner and bee-lining straight for the kitchen—the hurricane of everything that has passed today and the memories that still give me nightmares, spurring me on.

CHAPTER TEN

Caged birds accept each other but flight is what they long for.
~Tennessee Williams

I FINISH GIVING out food as quickly as I can and then after collecting any old trays, I ask Connie about clocking out. She told me that they know when I'm here and when I'm not and to leave at my appointed time. The minute that clock hit 4 a.m. my ass was out the door.

Now I'm sitting on the cold metal bench at the bus stop waiting for a bus that won't be here for another forty-five minutes. The town is still dark and quiet, except for the random person who has to be up before everyone else. Mostly mail and paper delivery people. There are deer in the park across from me; I can see their silhouettes against the backdrop of the early sky. Watching them I start to relax a little because their presence is a spot of peace after a hectic day.

Taking a deep cleansing breath, I almost relax completely, almost. I can see the squat little man with a mushroom on his head rooting around the garbage cans. To test it I cover my right eye. The purple haze lessens, but it's still present, which is something new. I can't full-on see the little guy anymore, but I can see a blurry image, a moving one. Sonofabitch it's infected my other eye. This—fucking… my thoughts sputter to a halt when Athena lands boldly on my lap and looks up at me her beak open, a look of alarm on her face.

"What?" I ask concerned. She's smart, there's no doubt about that, and something has upset her. Without a sound, she pecks at the hand covering my eye and cussing, I drop the hand to look at the cut from her sharp ass beak.

"Why'd you do that?" I demand, shooing her off my lap. She hops away from my hand only to land back on my lap. "Look, this shit is all kinds of messed up, Athena. There's no such thing as fairies and sexy vampires and their hot twins and… what the hell is wrong with me?"

Athena makes her caw-like laugh low in her throat and pokes my face right next to my weird eye, gently this time.

"Are you saying this shit is real?" Hell, why am I asking a bird something so important? Well, how is this different from any other day? At least, talking to the birds part.

Athena caws at me then looks towards the little man who is now standing just in front of me holding his mushroom hat in his hand.

"Begging your pardon, miss, but your companion is trying to explain a few things to you, but you're not under-standing her yet." He's a cute little thing, with a child's face and big brown eyes. Puppy dog eyes that make me want to lean down to pet his small head.

"Hi." Yep, I have the most fabulous people skills.

"Hello! My name is Jacaby, and your familiar says your name is Melantha. Strong name that, there's a lot of history and magic in that name. Is your mother one of the wee folks?" It's good to know that I'm not the only nervous chatter bug on the planet. I relax a bit more, as things in my mind start clicking into place.

I'm very familiar with the symptoms of schizophrenia. There aren't 3D hallucinations like this. Interacting with their environment on this type of level. I'm not experiencing mania of any kind, and my anxiety feels like normal anxiety to me. So, *when you have eliminated the impossible, whatever remains, however improbable, must be the truth.* Thank you, Sir Arthur Conan Doyle.

Yes, delusions can feel real, but there are other symptoms that I'm missing, important ones—inability to speak coherently coupled with disorganized or even catatonic behavior. The biggest being lack of pleasure in life and let me tell you when Vale kissed me there was definitely no lack of desire there. I have enough damn sense to know that as surreal as things are, they feel *real*.

I felt the smooth ridges of the scars on Min's frail body. My fingers grazed the bones through Gahna's too delicate skin because she's so malnourished that even her muscle tissue is degenerating. I smelled the stench of waste and unwashed bodies. Saw the bleariness of defeat in some of their eyes. There's no way my imagination cooked up that kind of suffering.

But come on? Wouldn't there be more internet buzz if these kinds of things exist?

"Miss Melantha?" Jacaby's voice breaks into my thoughts.

"I'm trying to decide if you're a symptom or not," I say.

"Symptom? Are you ill?" The concern on his face and in his voice isn't the kind you can fake. It's genuine and heartwarming and—

I'm so fucked.

"Something like that," then it hits me that he called Athena my familiar. "What do you mean familiar? I'm not a freaking witch, am I?" Although, if ever I decide to go along with believing all this crazy shit, a witch sounds kind of cool, other than the burning at the stake-thing. Not that I think they still do that, but who knows? None of what's happened to me today can be considered normal in any way shape or form. Even the cleaning part was weird. Something I didn't think was possible.

"She is a magical construct created for the Path Keeper. Until you started to see the real world, she'd have been invisible to you Miss Melantha. But now your magical eye is open," he says pointing at my right eye. He smiles again, and his dimples peek out. God, he's freaking adorable.

"If this," I point at the weird eye, "was gone. Would I stop seeing stuff?" Would I go back to the normal routine? Well, as normal as it can be.

Yeah, so ordinary that you talk to birds because you don't have any friends and have wet dreams about swimming in loaves of bread because you're so hungry, loser.

I think sometimes my subconscious hates me.

Jacaby laughs and twists his hat in his hands, "What is now seen can't be unseen. Why fight what you are?" He pops his hat on his head and gives me an elegant bow. "I'm off now. I need to fetch dinner for the little ones. Might I say that we are all glad you've come?" He turns and walks across the street, whistling while he walks. Little guy moves fast for having six-inch long legs.

Athena's rough laugh brings my attention back to her, still perched on my leg.

"What did you expect? Mental illness runs in my family. I have every right to question the existence of monsters and shit." She tilts her head to the side, and it makes me think she's rolling her eyes at me. I return the favor and lean my head back against the glass wall of the bus depot. Looking up at the cobwebs and what I'm pretty sure is chewed gum, or worse considering where I am, I run as much of the day through my head that I can.

An entire day of off the wall shit and yet I'm sitting here calm as a corpse. Sure, there's anxiety but nothing above what I experience on a daily basis. I'm tired, hell, I'm even a bit scared, but for the life of me, I can't find anything that screams delusions. I have nothing to blame for all this straight out of the TV shit, except that there's a good chance it's real.

Blowing out a breath, Athena clicks her beak at me for disturbing her. Absently, I stroke her back to apologize and close my eyes.

Am I really sitting here hoping that this is all a big delusion and that I'm lying somewhere in a room or on a park bench with a stupid smile on my face, catatonic?

Yes, and no. Yes, because I want to have the same stupid beliefs as everyone else, there's no such thing as fairies. No, because it's so freaking awesome to know that everything I imagined or dreamed about as a kid and hell, as an adult... is real!

They're real and stuck in that awful place to slowly die. Fuck.

The rumbling of the bus as it slowly lumbers up the road brings me out of my reverie, and I sit up with a deep, weary sigh. Athena flaps her wings at me and then takes off, a spot of black moving among the shadows cast by the impending sunrise. Her departure doesn't worry me. I'm confident she'll be waiting for me when I get home.

The bus jerks to a stop and I stand, stretching a little as I do. Thankfully, the ride will be short, and then I can sleep for the day. Sleep and let my mind shut the hell up for a while.

AN HOUR after I climbed into my bed, I'm still staring at the ceiling trying to get my brain to settle down enough to let me sleep. I'm tired, I worked hard—I need sleep! But no, my mind says fuck you instead. After the day I've had I should be a weeping mess with an armful of ice cream tubs and a bottle of vodka, yet I still feel relatively sane, no breakdowns and no tears even. And yes, part of me still wishes that it was all part of some fantasy my brain cooked up because I flipped my wig.

Logic tells me it's all true. Funny that logic is telling me that paranormal shit is real, that I'm working in a prison for fairies and dragons and hot as hell vampire guys. Well, one's a vampire for sure, Tavin is something else. I'm pretty sure he eats people or people like things. The two of them are identical, and yeah… both make my stomach do the Macarena. I can admit it without feeling stupid. I mean come on, they look like supermodels with perfect, lean bodies. Tavin was mostly covered in filth and other gross things the first time I met him, but could still pull off gorgeous. While even though Vale was an old man who had no teeth, at least in the beginning, he still made me feel things I'd rather not ever admit to out loud for an old dude. Now, it's worse.

God, I'm all fucked up for thinking about this instead of why I see fantastical shit.

Maybe I need to go out and attempt to socialize with relatively ordinary people? Maybe drink a little bit too much and dance around with some horny, desperate guy who thinks rubbing my shoulders with his smelly hands makes me hot? I mean, I've done it with less motivation than I have now.

Rubbing a hand down my face, I roll over again. Movement behind me brings me back around to look into Athena's black eyes.

"I feel like this is somehow your fault. This all started the minute I chased your feather." The look she's giving me makes me roll my eyes at her. "Yeah, you saved my life and all but still... you took me to the Unsylum where all the," I wave my hand around while I search my tired brain for the right word, "fucked-up laser vision shit works. I'm too tired to think of anything else."

Hopping towards me she gently pecks at my hair and lightly caws at me.

"Not that I don't appreciate the life-saving bit and the job, but that place makes me worry I've got the same issues as my Grandmother; that eventually, I'll completely lose my mind and off myself in the garage on Christmas Eve."

When Athena lowers her head and slowly moves it side to side, I roll off the other side of the bed onto the floor.

"Did you shake your head no?" I ask breathlessly. After all the shit I've seen today it's her shaking her head no that freaks me out? Just as slowly she moves her head up and then down. My chest tightens, and I force myself to take several deep breaths to stop the panic attack in its tracks. I know why her reactions—her *human* reactions—are freaking me out so bad. It's one thing if it's in a place that I'm unfamiliar with, out there in the world. Things change when it's in my sanctuary, my home.

This is the place I should be safe from the shit out *there.*

When the first hot tear slides down my cheek, I'm surprised. When more follow and loud, snotty sobs start, I rest my head on my knees and let it all out.

"I love your melons!" Loki, the Lord of random perversion, yells from his cage.

A snort escapes me and when a warm, feathered head

butts against my arm I lift my swollen eyes to look into Athena's eyes.

"This shit's all real, isn't it?" That slow nod is my answer.

Wiping my face with the sleeve of my bright pink pajamas, I climb to my feet and trudge into the bathroom to wash my face. This shows how put together I am, I'm taking the word of a bird that everything I'm seeing isn't merely a cluster of symptoms.

Crawling back in bed I pull my ragged teddy bear tight against me, hugging it like my life depends on it, I close my eyes and let sleep finally have me.

CHAPTER ELEVEN

Just remember it's the birds that's supposed to suffer, not the hunter.
   ~George W. Bush

THE NEXT AFTERNOON the ear cringing sound of all three of the boys squawking like roosters brings me out of the dreams that plagued me most of the night—dreams of iron cages and death. Rolling over I sit up and rest my elbows on my thighs.

"Shut up, you stupid mini-chickens," I mutter, cringing a little at my morning breath. With a grimace, I climb to my sore feet and stagger into the bathroom.

When the toilet flushes a few minutes later, it drowns out the ruckus of the bird brats chirping obscenities and protests at me from the other room. Continuing to ignore their complaints—they were fed and watered before I went to sleep, they're just spoiled—I bathe my face in ice cold water then start brushing my teeth. I'm tired, but it's more of the soul weary kind than the physical and in my case, they happen to be connected.

Looking at my face in the mirror draws a gasp of surprise out of me, the toothbrush falls into the sink with a plastic clink and toothpaste flies all over the place.

"What the fuck?" I exclaim, my hand going instantly to my right eye. My goddamn glowing right eye. The swirling of fire and ice move together like a frozen slushie around the pupil.

The slit pupil that does not belong in my eyeball!

"What the fuck?" I ask my fucked-up-eyeball reflection, again.

"Shove it down your throat, whore!" Willis screeches, breaking the staring contest with myself. That's his signal of an impending temper tantrum, and a peek at the vocabulary he picked up from Loki. With one last look in the mirror at my pale face and the glowing globe that's another brick in the wall of weirdness in my life, I go out to stand in front of him. The little bald asshole is on the rope closest to the bathroom, giving me a dirty look with his chicken wings pushed up and out.

"Dude I could flick you on the beak and break the annoying thing," I look over at his full water and food dish, "If you're too impatient to wait for me then go eat your food in the full freaking dish, you mouthy little bastard." Opening his beak, he hisses at me. "You can wait, Willis."

It's hard to stay mad at his naked ass though, he looks like a raw rotisserie chicken. A laugh escapes me, and I shake my head as I work on getting dressed and ready for work. It's already after two o'clock, and I still must take care of the buttheads and find a way to fix my eye. Or cover it or something. A light bulb goes off in my slow brain, hurrying to the small cabinet I call a closet, I dig through the myriad of bags and tubs in it until I find one marked 'medical.'

With a noise of triumph, I tear it open and dig through it until I find the pack of sterile eye patches and medical tape. Going back into the bathroom I cover the fucked eye and look at the mess of tape crisscrossing my face in the mirror.

"What are you staring at?" I say to my reflection, "It's covered which means I won't see any more magical shit and no one else can see how *not* human it is. "Denial isn't just a river, Mel. It's a way of life." I whisper at my reflection before maturely sticking my tongue out.

High on the false sense of security—that I'm fully aware will crash onto my head at some point, I hum happily while taking care of the now silent trio of birds. Athena is quietly watching me—no, judging me—from the windowsill of the miraculously closed window, thank God because it's cold outside. Although, I have no idea how she's closing it and I really—since I'm all about denial—don't want to know. I offer her some bird seed and while, for the first few seconds, she looks at me like I'm crazy—which is probably very accurate—she still starts randomly pecking at it. Good girl knows that it's that or nothing.

At least, until we get to the Unsylum, somehow, I managed to luck out enough to get free food there, it's the only reason I'm not panicking and rushing out the door to get a dollar burger or something from the gas station. But that kind of food is desperate food, especially when it comes to the food from the local ones here, you're playing Russian roulette with E.coli. I'm not sure that the employee bathrooms at work are somewhere that I want to spend any lengthy amount of time as a result of chancing the food. They're super clean but creepy as hell. I felt like someone was watching me while I was there yesterday. That's an awful feeling to have when you're at your most vulnerable. If someone suddenly attacked, I'd pee all over them and that's not cool.

Besides, eating before work would be great, but I won't starve to death before my first break, and Connie gives massive portions. Although food isn't my most urgent desire, coffee is, and I'm not sure if I get coffee free or not. It's probably a better idea if I stop somewhere on the way and grab a cup, but that would mean walking, and that will delay me longer than I have. Being late is a chance I can't take, but I really need something to kick my ass into gear. I love tea but I'm not sure it'll do it for me today.

As I move around the room, I avoid looking into the small wall mirror above the sink, allowing myself to stay in my fake happy zone. Fighting with the dented door of my apartment sized dryer makes me want coffee even more. Putting one socked foot on the frame, I pull with both hands. It gives with a suddenness that sends me back on my ass.

"Seriously, you little jerks?" I ask as all three of the little shit birds cackle in their form of laughter.

Grumbling about my sore butt, I climb to my feet and put on my wrinkled uniform. Frowning I look down at the disaster that leaving it in the dryer all night created. It smells good, but have some white fuzz here and there on it and coupled with the wrinkles, it looks slept it in. Great, I look like someone's unwanted drunk cousin. Unfortunately, there's nothing I can do about it. I don't have an iron; usually I'd throw them back in the dryer for ten minutes.

Looking at my phone, I see that I don't have time for that. Figures.

Willis starts throwing insults at me again. I stop long enough to glare at him to say, "Shut up, before I put you on a kabob where you belong." He instantly shuts up and looks at me like a kicked puppy. He's such an ungrateful bird, but even as I think that I reach out to gently pat his head. Of course, I get bitten, but still.

Rechecking the time, I start rushing around to get the shit I need to get done, done. I pet each one of the guys, even the mouthy-biter, grab my purse and umbrella—because one rainy walk was enough for me, and head out the door. When I briefly look back as I walk by the main house my Mom waves at me from the large picture window in the front. Pausing I smile and wave back, I do love her—I don't want her to see how big of a loser her only child is.

The absolute, irreversible truth is, I'm not ashamed of her —I'm ashamed of me.

I realize the minute she notices the eye-patch, so I turn away before she can come outside and mother-hen me. I jog towards the bus stop, the bus runs at three and doesn't run again until six so I have to catch this one or I'm walking to work, and I don't want to do that shit again. Especially since my shoes have seen better days, I'm using maxi-pads instead of insoles. Who in the world pays twenty bucks for rubber inserts when you can use these pads for way less cost… also, way less comfort but we'll call it semantics for now.

Once I'm safely on the bus, I sigh and sink down into the seat. I'll look pitifully at Connie. She might fall for it and supply me caffeinated energy for the day. Plan in mind, I check the patch and relax for a little while—the foreboding feeling that today is going to be one I always remember dogging my heels.

CHAPTER TWELVE

The bird thinks it's a favor to give the fish a lift in the air.
~Rabindranath Tagore

THAT DARK FEELING follows me through the door, past the secretary who gives me a dismissive look and shakes her head, and into the gloomy lounge where I stash my purse. I hurry out of the room before the breathing things I hear come out of whatever shadow or hole they're hiding in. The patch isn't nearly as effective as I hoped, I can still see shit—everywhere. It's not as vivid, and some things I know are missing but the people—well, creatures—don't look as human as they did before Vale hocked a loogie in my eyeball. The purple haze is missing but I'm pretty sure that eventually, I'll see it all in my left eye too and that this is some stop-gap measure that's only temporary and makes me look like a moron.

The moron part is proven correct when Brett spots me.

With a malicious smile on his face, he beelines right towards me and gives me a rough shoulder bump. Side-stepping to keep my balance, I put a few feet of distance between us and try to ignore him. Maybe he'll go away if I say nothing? Isn't that the right way to deal with a bully?

Although, it's never worked as far as I know. Usually, it makes them hit you harder.

My worry is proven correct when something hard and pointy hits me on the left side of my face, immediately blinding me in my left eye. I teeter backward against the wall, sliding down it as I furiously rub my watering eye to try and make the stars marring my vision clear. That motherfucker hit me!

"What the fuck, Brett?" I demand, trying to look at him through the Niagara Falls blurring my eye.

"Can't take a joke, little girl?" I'm going to punch him right in his big fucking mouth, that's what's going to happen. The minute I can stand without falling back over that is. The skin on my face is doing that hot, cold thing it does when you're hit by someone's damn elbow hard enough to know you're nearly unconscious. I can feel my cheek and eye swelling, I can feel the hot blood on my lips, taste its coppery tang on my tongue. Just how hard did he freaking hit me?

In most places I've worked someone hitting you like that would immediately get them fired, probably arrested. At best you'd hope for some justice. Here? I don't think that's the case, at all. Brett's done this before. I bet they all have. It would explain why there's no one working this job.

Wait, didn't Vale say he ate my predecessor? Do I believe that he did? Why don't I feel like I'd meet the same fate? Honestly, my gut tells me Brett, and his ilk are more likely to hurt me than other people... creatures, here. So why the hell am I still here? Why did I get up and come here knowing that this place is fucking whacked?

Money. Yes, that's mostly it, but not the only reason.

"You have a strong, kind heart, don't let them cut it out, Mel." The girl I shared my sandwich with says from above me. Rubbing the heel of my hand in my eye, I clear it up enough to look at her. She looks better today, still wearing the cleaner nightgown I put on her yesterday.

A bit embarrassed about the entire thing I climb to my feet and only wobble a little once I'm standing. Leaning my hand against the wall, I glance at Brett who's smirking and either ignoring the girl or not seeing her. When she turns her head to look at him, her hair whips around her shoulders like little pissed off snakes. It's a bit awesome, I can't deny it—her upper lip curls exposing some piranha looking teeth. I almost wish I had teeth like that; then I could bite the assholes face off.

Feeling a smile tickling the edge of my mouth, I swipe a hand over it to make it stay hidden. If I smile Brett might take that as an invitation to hit me again and I can't have that. I'll break his fucking face if he hits me again. Now I have to decide if I'm going to try and go to whatever management this place has and report him.

"It won't do you any good. Find comfort in the fact that justice will find him before the day ends," she says, walking towards the cafeteria. After a moment of indecision, I follow her. I want coffee anyhow and, Connie might feel enough pity for me now to give it to me.

"What's your name?" I ask her. She pauses and looks over her shoulder at me surprised before continuing.

"Marigold."

"That's a pretty name. I can honestly say I've never met someone with it before."

"Most people name their livestock Marigold, I hate my name."

Well, then I don't know what to say to that. I'm not a big fan of mine either. Speaking of mine, I open my mouth to tell her and realize that she's already used it. My mouth snaps shut, and I focus on ignoring the walls that I can now see breathing again.

Yeah, this patch is super effective.

"You already know mine. I'm not a fan of it either." See, I'm a nervous chatterer. I don't give into it every single time but this girl—who is probably an ancient goddess from some island that sank in the ocean or got eaten by a volcano—makes me nervous. It's not that I'm afraid, but it's a close thing that skitters along my skin. I feel like I should be scared, if that makes sense? It's incredibly similar to Vale and Tavin—minus the mind-fucked attraction thing I've got going for them.

"Your name is old and rare. Do you know the meaning of it?" Her question brings me out of my self-flagellation for being attracted to 'patients,' or monsters or whatever they are.

"No. My Mom said that it was the only request that my Dad had concerning me." The absolute truth, or at least what she told me.

"It means 'dark flower,' in my culture. It's a sacred name reserved for priestesses and guardians." She stops directly in front of the cafeteria doors and turns to me. "Covering the eye won't change anything. Eventually the other will open as wide, and there'll be no more hiding. But," she pats my arm in an awkward comforting way. I have a feeling that she doesn't comfort anyone often. "I understand why you're doing it. Growing up as a human has infected you with their humanness. But it's not that taint that's keeping you here now. It's the magic pulling at you, the magic you were born with," she taps her bottom lip with a finger before continuing, "You have good instincts, they'll steer you in the right direction, listen to them instead of that false humanity."

Okay, then.

"Thanks, I think?"

"Go get your energy soup, avoid the fake fairy, he'll be dealt with soon enough." With a final pat, she walks by me slowly down the hallway towards the elevator.

What the hell just happened?

Almost like it's pre-planned, the door swings open and Connie stands in the doorway her arms crossed, her eyes on the left side of my face and the horns I've seen before flickering in and out of existence. She looks angry.

"Coffee?" I ask stupidly.

Her frown melts into a smile, a grumpy but still a nice one. She grabs my arm and yanks me into the kitchen.

Yes! Coffee!

❦

"You're the only person I've ever seen hum while they eat," Connie muses, sipping her tea while watching me eat the second bowl of oatmeal. With a shrug I smile up at her and keep eating, I can't help it, this is the best oatmeal I've ever had. Apples and cinnamon and there's even some brown sugar mixed in there. It's like having a warm, yummy party in my mouth and I can't help but hum in happiness. Food is one of the great loves of my life.

"Why are you wearing that ridiculous thing on your face?" she asks.

Scraping the last bit of oatmeal out of the bowl I let the spoon fall into it with a metallic clang and push it to the side. Sitting back in the chair with a full stomach and a hot cup of coffee in my hand I smile again.

"It keeps things normal," I say in response.

"If you say so," I swear she rolls her eyes. "As soon as you finish your coffee, the trays are ready for you, and there's a snack in there for when you're in between floors. A couple of sodas too." Without another word she turns and goes back to the kitchen. Taking an experimental sip of my coffee, I find that it's not scalding hot anymore and chug it. I don't want to get behind today.

Grabbing the food cart, I start whistling as I push it out the door towards the first-floor rooms. Looking at the schedule posted on the side of the pushcart I see that Vale is first again. I can freely admit that I'm looking forward to seeing him and well, that makes me feel odd. A lot of things in this place makes me feel that way.

Especially warnings from little, old girls who are ancient volcano virgin sacrifices or some shit. When I look at her, that's exactly where my brain goes. Old, scary and she probably eats people too. Why else have piranha teeth? Of course, I'd rather none of them consume me. That would totally suck.

I genuinely don't think they will. How fucked up is that?

I do dumb shit sometimes. I think it's something everyone is guilty of, but I'm not an actual idiot—most of the time. Last night I had no choice but to admit that this shit I'm seeing is one-hundred percent real, especially after googling every symptom of every single mental illness where one hallucinates. Yeah, I'm a bit off, but I'm not schizophrenic. There's something else going on here. There has to be. Other than the little dude Jacaby at the bus stop, I didn't see one paranormal thing at home—besides Athena nodding and appearing more human-like every time she looks at me. I swear if she turns into some Celtic chick with a chip on her shoulder I'm moving far, far away. I'll become a beach bum and eat sushi or something.

Sushi being whatever I can pull out of the garbage can at the bazillion restaurants along the beach.

Yeah, I don't have schizophrenia, but I'm not right in the head, not at all. I'm just not mentally ill enough to push this all off as symptoms. I wish that I could, oh, how I wish.

"Hit him again you idiot!" The yelled words yanked me right out of my reverie. I peek around the cart and see two of the guards standing outside of Vale's room. They look like they're rooting for their home team at the football game. Why would they be—oh, hell no.

Leaving the cart in the middle of the hallway, I run to them and push the bigger one out of the way. Inside Vale stands half-naked, covered in blood—like saturated in the shit—being circled by two of the winged, fake fairies as Marigold calls them, like he's some kind of trapped animal.

That's not too far off the mark, is it?

"What are you doing?" I demand, pushing my way past the other two to stand in between them and Vale. "What kind of losers are you to pick on someone who can't defend themselves?" I yell.

"He ate Brett!" The one closest to me yells pointing at Vale behind me, who chuckles close to my ear. When did he step so close? I look at him over my shoulder. He's standing so close to me that he could kiss me if he wanted to, without moving.

"Get out, now. Or I swear I'll open every door on the third floor." I have no idea where I came up with the threat, but it works. With looks of abject hatred, they both turn and leave the room. I'm only partially surprised when the door slams shut and is locked.

"You like him so much stay in there and let him eat you." The one in the too tight uniform says through the tray slot.

"Well, that's fun." I turn to him and ask, "Why did you eat Brett?" I head into the bathroom to get something to clean him up with. "I thought you did the whole blood drinking thing?" I ask as nonchalantly as I'm able. I freely admit that I pulled it off better than I expected. In fact, I kind of want to lock myself in the bathroom and have a bit of a good cry.

Now that I've accepted that it's all real, I can take off this stupid patch. I rip it off, taking some long eyebrow hairs with it, and toss it in the garbage can. Wearing it was a bit dumb anyhow, denial never works. Everything eventually collapses in on your head, and you have no choice but to accept life for what it is.

Shit, usually it's shit.

"Why did you hide the gift you were given?" It's the first thing Vale asks me when I leave the bathroom, wet washcloth in hand. I keep my head down and focus on the mess he's covered in. I'm pretty sure some of the blood is his, but the wounds are gone.

"I saw all kinds of shit, Vale."

"You saw the truth," his voice is soft, almost chiding. He isn't happy I covered my eye.

"Maybe, but it was your truth, not mine." Finally, I look up into his eyes and find myself caught there like a fat lady bug in a big spider's web. Stuck hard-core with every movement more deeply entangling me.

"That's not the case any longer." Truth, more truth and nothing but the truth.

Subject change. "You really ate him?"

He leans down and smiles his no longer toothless smile, "Every worthless bit of him."

"He—how?" I sputter out nervously but not the run-away kind. More in lean forward and kiss him and hope there aren't pieces of Brett stuck in his teeth. That image cools the moment, and I pull away. I toss the cloth at him and laugh a little when it slides down his chest to land on the floor with a wet plop.

"Where are those inhuman reflexes?" That teasing smile touches his lips again, and I shiver. Man, that thing is deadly.

"You watched its progress, did you not?" He did it on purpose? What a sneaky move. Also, a funny one which my laughter proves. Shaking my head at the absurdity of this situation I pick up the mess of his room and dig the keys out of my pocket. The locks open from both sides, so I'm not sure what tweedle-dick and tweedle-dumbass thought by locking me in here.

"You requested that I only eat bad guys, Mel."

"I can't deny that. I'm not sure that him smacking me in the head with his elbow was a good enough reason to eat him though."

This time Vale snorts, "Your encounter with him wasn't the only reason for his death, Mel."

Well, now I feel like an idiot who put way too much worth on myself. What the hell was I thinking? Of course, there were other reasons. These guards torture the people in this place.

"Since you gave of yourself, I'm finally returning to my natural state. Feeding on him will hasten that along. Not as quickly as the ambrosia you gave me though." I'm pretty sure that last part is him trying to mollify me—the gallant turd. Having nothing to say, since I seem to be full of dumbassery, I push open the door and get the cart.

Digging out Vale's breakfast, I look both directions down the hallway before using the sharp edge of the small knife on the keychain and cut my finger. Compared to a full body of blood, this isn't much but my instincts—the annoying things —are pushing me to do it. Hell, I didn't fully realize what I was doing until I felt the sting of the blade.

Yeah. I drank the Kool-Aid. In fact, I gulped that shit down and am now bathing it. Heaven help me.

Vale meets me at the door, and there's laughter dancing in

his eyes. Eyes that hold mine steadily while he drinks the shake I hand him. This time he licks his lips to catch the last drops and then gives me the empty cup.

"Thank you for your gift. I grow stronger from it." Then he winks at me, like full on flirty wink.

If my panties were capable of melting, they'd have puddled in my beat-up sneakers right then. Unable to stop myself I look down and then with a full-on blush look back up into his laughing face.

"I still think there's a chance I'm in some catatonic state and imagining this entire thing because I watched too much TV as a kid." Yesterday, I'd have meant it, but now it's half-hearted at best. I've always been an odd duck. My Mom used to freak out when I talked about magic and monsters as a kid —like hard-core freak out.

Is this why? Does she know something about all this fuckery?

"You and I both know that no matter how shaky you are on your new legs, you're still standing." My blank look makes him smile. "You're full of shit and know that this is all happening." Okay, that's more my language. And he's right. I'm way too calm about all of this. It's almost like I finally found the place I'm supposed to be.

We'll let the irony about it being an asylum pass.

CHAPTER THIRTEEN

No one is free, even the birds are chained to the sky.
~Bob Dylan

TWO WEEKS LATER, I'm still extraordinarily calm about the entire mess, and still employed there—something that's a shocker in itself. The Unsylum seems to get stranger every single day, but I genuinely enjoy the people there. Except for the guards, they're never ending assholes, especially the old ones. Last week all those I'm familiar with vanished on the same day. At the beginning of my shift, while I was talking to Marigold—who wanders the Unsylum freely—about how to raise a talking duck, they were nervous and agitated. Even meaner than their typical douchebag standard on top of it. I'm pretty sure I was tripped like fifty times in two-hours, but by the end of my shift, they were gone.

Whether they ended up in someone's digestive tract, I

don't know. What I do know is that the peace and quiet from their absence was worth every single guilty feeling about it. Work was great for two whole days. People were out of their rooms walking around and enjoying themselves, maybe for the first time in years. As it always goes, good things always come to an end. Whoever manages this place decided that bringing in new Fake Fairies—that's what the Unsylum folks call them—was a good idea. Their whole creation process is fascinating to me, but so far, I've not been given in-depth explanations about any of it.

That's supposed to end today.

Since Vale and I talk throughout a good part of the day, every day, I'm glad he's finally agreed to tell me whatever doom and gloom bullshit is going on here. I asked Tavin, but he isn't really a talker, not like Vale is anyhow, and although I feel an attraction toward him—it's not quite what I feel for Vale—muted almost, but undeniably still there.

How fucking weird am I?

Weird enough that I still manage to feel guilty for every second of attraction I have for them but not enough to make me stop being around them. And no one, not even Marigold, will answer any questions I have about the twins, not even the twins themselves. I sense a massive secret there, and it annoys the crap out of me that no one will tell me anything. I mean, if it were a secret that had no impact on me at all, I'm nosy enough to want to know but not so much so that it'd bother me *not* knowing. In this case, I think it *is* about me or has something to do with me, which means I need to know. All their stupid games aside, it'd be nice to have some honesty from them that didn't come with some crappy, *when you're ready* line.

I should get a large, shiny medal awarded to me for making it through this situation. Maybe even one of those wine gift baskets, heavy on the wine. I've accepted that there are things that go bump in the night, rather eloquently, if I might say so. Well, if you leave out the *almost* panic attacks, damn near constant doubt and the slim, ever-shrinking hope that I was just mentally ill. That's a win in my book; the key word is almost.

However, the secrets being kept from me upset me more than accepting that paranormal shit exists. Their existence is like having a pointy sesame seed stuck between your teeth rubbing a sore spot on your gums. No matter how many times you poke at it with your tongue, or brush your teeth—hell, even take some floss to it, it resolves nothing. All the seed does is dig deeper into your aching gums and makes everything ten times worse. If I really wanted to, I could compare it to a cactus spine or a tick. A greedy, deep digging tick.

With Lyme's Disease.

Forcing my thoughts away from the image that cooks up in my brain, I realize that I enjoy coming to work, not because of the comfort of having a job or even the security of a steady paycheck, simply because I like them. But, as far as the perks go, I've managed to get a real bed, I'm saving up for an apartment, and I paid my mom back for the first time in a decade. The satisfaction from that is one of the most freeing feelings I've ever had in my life. I plan on working to keep it that way or at least until they find some fucked up way to fire me here.

I wave to Bob the Blob—yes, I named him that and I'm fully aware that it has no originality at all, but the poor thing didn't have a name, just a creature tag. Which is what the Fake Fairies register them under, creature tags. It's a blatant form of racism… no, speciesism, if I've ever seen one. Not only are they some kind of prisoners or something in this place, but they're also demeaned in such a way they don't get names. Come to find out, the names on the tray lists Connie gives me, she puts on there—not the management. She said it's her one way to recognize them for the special people they are. Which, besides the apparent humanity—fairymanity, whatever—struck me as an odd turn of phrase and so I asked her. I mean, that's a dangled carrot if I ever saw one. Of course, she smiled and turned away to stir her gigantic soup pot. I swear they're torturing me for fun with the mysteries and allusions. All around me, I get hints about how things are, but no one gives me any reliable information. Especially from Vale, all I get from him is, *I'm waiting for you to blossom.*

What the hell is he waiting for me to blossom into? A fucking butterfly?

I see fantastical crap daily—hell, every damn *minute* and I have conversations with two-inch tall *real* fairies about hair conditioner. How have I not 'blossomed' enough to find out what the hell is going on here? I'm not a fan of vague bullshit. I'm that person that would pass over all the what if's and know how's and skip to the end of the story of life, versus wading through six feet of shit to only end up dead because of something they didn't tell me.

"You think too hard about stupid things at times, Mel." Marigold's voice beside me might no longer startles me as it did before, but there's still a small zing of apprehension. Every single time.

"How are you today, Marigold?" It's my small payback. She prefers that I call her Mari.

"Well, I suppose. The garden is waking up again, you should go find it one day soon," she says, then promptly turns and walks off. She reminds me of a psycho version of that cricket from all the mouse movies. You know the ones. M-I-C-blah, blah, blah.

I stroll into Tavin's room who gives me a knowing look that annoys me ten ways to Sunday.

"Patience is a virtue for a reason," Tavin chides from

where he's lounging, chainless now, on his bed watching me like an owl watches the dumb, slow mouse.

One day I'm pretty sure he's going to sink those teeth into me. What I'm not entirely sure of, is in what way. His smile widens and my stomach flutters. Honestly, I've admitted—to myself only—I'm sexually attracted to the twins, monsters or not. They have the effect of making my womb cry for me to yank my clothes off and say, *take me now, I'm fertile.*

"Patience doesn't help you enjoy your life. It merely makes getting the things you want to take longer." His laugh is deep and infectious. I laugh with him. "Are you sure the two of you don't read minds?"

"Yes, we can smell and see how you feel. No mind-reading needed." He leans forward, and the shirt on him gapes open showing off the pale skin covering that tight, yummy—Christ, Mel get ahold of yourself. *The wayward path you're currently going down is leading you to his lap.* I bitch at myself, trying to stop the tidal wave of hormones that subconsciously made me move a step closer to him. God, I'm just as bad with Vale, maybe even worse because that man flirts so effortlessly, I don't even realize how charmed I am until I'm practically licking his... face.

Sure. Face.

"Where do you go off to when your eyes glaze over, and your mouth hangs open?" His question makes me jerk right out of my reverie about licking things, and my mouth snaps shut. Giving him a dirty look, I grab his laundry and leave, the rude man. Saying my eyes glaze over and my mouth hangs open. That's rude to say to a lady.

Not that I'm a lady.

AFTER I'M FINISHED with the third floor, I wander around to

find a hidey-hole to take my lunch in. The residents them-selves always manage to find me, which is fine most of the time, it's the guards I'm trying to avoid. I'm not exaggerating when I say they're assholes, all of them. The last time they found me they took my sandwich and stomped on it. Before that, they wastefully dumped that delicious homemade tomato soup on my head. So, I walked around all day in a uniform stained with what looked like not-tomato soup, smelling like a rotten vegetable garden.

A feeling of awareness lassoes me right around the gut and tugs hard. Stopping in my tracks, I turn towards its source and find myself facing a dusty old door. It's another iron one—they have a thing for them here—but this one hasn't been used for a long time. The hinges are rusted, and the doorknob is hanging by one screw.

With the usual aplomb I show here, reckless and stupid mostly, I grab it and yank. Unsurprisingly, it comes off in my hand. Annoyed, I try to get it to reattach, you know—because that's magically going to happen. To properly communicate my desire to get it to go in the hole, I bang the knob against it a few times. Resting my hand against the door, I pull it back when a sharp pain shoots through my palm. Looking at it I see a single drop of blood welled up on it. I eye the door that bit me. There's a smear of red outlined by what looks like my palm print.

Leaning closer I hold my hand up to the spot and push it flat against the smooth metal of the door. A soothing warmth suffuses my hand right before iron claws of pain reach up and grab my entire body locking me against the door. Yelling, I try to pull my hand away and only end up slapping the door with my other hand and screaming bloody murder at the damn thing.

"Give me my damn hand back! Why does it always have to be about blood?" I yell at the door—a wave of hot air slams into my face pushing my eyes shut. Another wave stings my cheeks and tears my hair from its loose band. The next wave is a continuous stream that makes my eyes water from the force of it. With tears streaming down my face I try to turn my head away enough to open them and see what the hell is going on.

Just as I'm about to accomplish this, the wind stops as suddenly as it began. Using my sleeve to wipe the moisture from my face I give the door the dirtiest look I have in my arsenal and this time when I pull on my hand it comes away with no problems, sending me back into a windmilling mess, yet I somehow manage to catch myself before I hit the hard floor.

The handprint on the door, my handprint, begins to pulse a bright white. The rhythm is unmistakable as anything other than a heartbeat. Curious despite myself, I rest my hand over my chest and discover that it matches mine identically.

Did I honestly expect it to be a standard door?

"Now what?" I ask the empty hallway. The response to my question is for the door to click and open a few inches. "Hmph." I turn and look for the lunch bag that I dropped when the door tried to eat my hand. My footprint stands out from the top of the bag. I snatch it off the ground anyhow. Food is too precious to waste, stepped on or not.

With a deep breath for bravery—something that my stupidity likes to hide behind—I push on the door, and it opens as easily as a brand new one. Muttering a few insults at the door, because you know, doors care so very much about what we think of them, I step into the dark room.

The stupidity has chosen to now run in front of the bravery.

With a whoosh sound, the lights flare on. A single step backward brings me up against the door frame. The room...

the room is everything an old hidden place in my imagination should be. There's a skull on the old secretary desk, with a freaking melting candle on it! Books line the walls; there's even a podium with an open book on it that, from here, looks authentically old and creepy. There are dust bunnies and spider webs everywhere, giving this room every single touch of Addam's Family library that it can.

"I thought it would take you forever to find this place. Sometimes you're so damn slow, Mel." The female's voice startles me so much I throw the lunch bag towards the source. The harsh caw of Athena makes me almost regret it, almost.

"Thanks, Athena, you're so supportive," I answer her, not surprised she's talking to me. Jacaby told me weeks ago that she talked and well, a talking bird isn't the oddest thing I've come across in this place.

Not by a long shot.

"I have to admit. I'm rather proud of you. You've accepted this with more composure than I expected. You've even limited your melt downs to weekly instead of nightly," she teases. I follow her voice to find that she's perched on an old golden cage that's torn open. I'm pretty sure that whatever was in it broke out instead of something breaking in.

"Oh, thanks," I point towards the hole in the cage, "Was that your former home?"

"Once. The former master betrayed this place, and I had no choice but to flee," she says with sadness lacing her words. This master was someone she cared about.

"I'm sorry."

She hops down to the desk and rummages around in the mess of things on top of it. I can hear her muttering to herself and cover my mouth to hide my smile. She sounds like I imagined her to. Her voice is smoky and similar to that lady on TV who does the wine commercials—the voice of a phone-sex operator in the body of a bird.

I giggle.

"I'm glad you're so entertained, Mel. Here," she flaps over to me and drops something heavy down the front of my shirt. Rolling my eyes at her, I reach in between my boobs and find my hand filled with warm metal.

"I promise that if this thing bites me, I'm going to make you eat it," I threaten, and pull it, reluctantly, out of my shirt to examine it.

In my hand is a golden amulet about the size of my palm. There is a ring of white stones—probably diamonds—set in it, with the center holding a large eight sided gem that's the color of flame. It's beautiful.

"That's yours," Athena says.

"This thing has to be worth a fortune. I can't take this," I insist.

"Mel, everything in this room is yours. You can take whatever you want."

Blinking a few times, I stare at her and say, "I'm sorry, what?"

"You're the Path Keeper. This is your room. This place—the Unsylum, is the Path."

I blink a few more times, trying to process. "Try again, bird."

"Pah, don't get mad about it. Here," she hops over to the podium, "this is your… guidebook of sorts. Read it, and you'll get many of the answers you seek."

"Okay, Athena…let's take it down one more level of dumb. You're saying that the Unsylum is a path?" She nods. "To where?"

"Everywhere. This is the doorway to all worlds. The magic users that have entrapped it and its guests inside are not the rightful heirs to it. When my former master deserted his post out of cowardice," this time there's anger mixed in with the sadness, "he left a vacuum of power that the witches and wizards from the Runin Realm took advantage of. Go on, read, it's all there in the book and will take a lot less time to read than for me to explain."

I almost push her, almost, but I feel like it's more that she doesn't want to talk about the person who she called master than her being lazy. No one likes to talk about something that hurts them.

"So, there's a shit ton of other worlds—which even science says is possible, so I don't feel too crazy accepting that—but the whole me being the Path Keeper thing. I suck at keeping plants alive how can I—"

Athena cuts me off, "You are one of the most compassionate people I've ever seen when it comes to caring for things. Did you forget I know about those three idiots you're caring for? What about what you've done for the inhabitants of this place?"

Well, then.

I open my mouth and she interrupts me again, "Don't even say it, Mel. You've known for a while now that there's a reason you're here, you just like playing stupid because it suits you." My mouth shuts, and I sit down in the chair that immediately collapses under my weight.

Laying on the dirty floor, I cover my face with my hands and laugh. What else can I do? The last few weeks of my life have been like some traumatic, never-ending, acid trip. But it's been one helluva trip. This is the icing on the cake, her telling me that I'm some keeper of a path thing. The thought of being responsible for anyone other than myself or the birds... that freaks me out more than a talking birds and breathing walls. My laughter takes on the edge of hysteria. What the fuck has happened to my life?

"Has she completely lost her mind this time?" Vale's deep

voice cuts right through the room and silences me immediately. Vale left his room? Rolling towards the door, I look up at him as he crosses the room—strolls really—his hands tucked in the pockets of a pair of jeans that I've never seen him in, a plain white t-shirt stretched across his lean frame... goddamn that man is fine.

I can't believe I'm laying on the floor contemplating throwing water on him to the soundtrack of Magic Mike.

Rolling onto my back again I cover my face with both hands this time.

"Have you told her, familiar?" he asks.

"Her being on the floor should be your answer," Athena answers, amusement thick in her voice.

"Everything?" His voice is closer now, and I swear I can feel his body heat.

"No, if that were the case, I'm sure she'd have tried to jump off the roof or run home by now."

Oh, shit, how bad is it that she thinks I'd freak out in those ways? Lifting my hands off my face, I look up into the bright eyes of Vale. Laughter is dancing in their hypnotic depths, but there's something darker, deeper there too. I shiver.

Yeah, Tavin isn't the only one whose teeth are sharp. The reaction I have to Vale is more visceral. And confusing, so confusing that I roll the opposite direction from him and climb to my feet. Wiping my dirty hands on my already filthy uniform, I cross to look at the book on the podium, mostly to avoid looking at Vale.

His hair is in a long braid, tossed casually over his shoulder, and I curl my fingers into my palm to keep myself from being a moron and reaching out to touch it. I already know his hair feels like strands of thick silk. It's textured in such a way that you want to rub it all over your body, like a weirdo. Forcing myself to look down, away from the knowing light in his eyes I manage to somehow read the first page of the book in front of me.

If you're reading this, then the former Keeper has passed on. Well, that isn't foreboding or anything, is it? Intrigued, I keep reading.

These words are the sacred writings for the Path Keeper. Always keep control of the Path, never fail in your task. If it is taken, take it back. This means you, Melantha. Get your finger out of your ear and read this book. Read it because your life—their lives—depend on it.

I slam the book shut after I stop itching my ear with my finger.

"Mel, is it that hard to believe you're important?"

"I'm not important, I've never been important—this is just…" My words sputter to a choked end. Gripping the edges of the podium, I take several deep, bracing breaths. No, I'm not important but the drive to read this book is a fucking *need.*

"More untrue words have never been spoken. For ten years I've sat here, pieces of myself scattered to the chaos of the chained Unsylum, waiting for you, Mel." His hands are firm but surprisingly gentle as he pries my hands off the podium and grasps them in his warm ones. "You may ask your questions, and I'll give you the answers that I have."

"What do you mean pieces of yourself?" That's not the question I wanted to ask, but I'll roll with it.

"For every part of me they remove, a duplicate or a twin of me forms. I see through all of them, I *am* all of them but because I'm in pieces, the main part of me is weakened."

Blink. Blink. Blink.

"Yes, Tavin is a piece of me," he answers my unspoken question.

"So—uh—like, that's you talking through him?"

A chorus of voices answer me, "I am he. He is I. We are

him. But split apart, hollow without our center." The multitude of voices sends my gaze flicking around. Tavin stands in the doorway, beside him yet another Vale look alike, one I don't recall seeing. Behind him a smaller, childlike version and on the other side of him yet another one, young but not quite a child. Vale catches me when I try to sit down in the broken chair again.

"Mel. Shake it off. There's no time for you to have an emotional crisis. Ask your questions, my time here is limited, soon I will need to return to that foul room and wait for them to turn their eyes away again. Only here can I give you the answers you seek but ask now!"

Perhaps it's the urgency of his tone, or maybe it's the clawing panic that I'm barely holding at bay. Maybe even more than anything it's the sense that once I get these answers, I'll be in the place I need to be.

"How do you become one again?" And as I ask it a part of me is a little sad that Tavin might not be here one day. The persona, because I know that's what it is now, that is Tavin smiles at me, and I see now that it's Vale looking out of those eyes at me.

It always has been.

"That one is easy," Vale says, pulling my attention back to the main him—that's so weird to think that. His smile is wide and pointy, putting a sexual edge to all those teeth, and like he's announcing the next president, he says, "I fuck you."

"Oh, that's all. A bit of stabby and grabby… and somehow my vagina sucks all those people in and spits out a whole you. Yep. That sounds fantastic," I mutter as the room starts to spin—the black spots hovering on the outer circle of my vision crowd in. The lightheadedness hits me like a truck, and the last thing I see is Vale's surprised face as his hands lift to catch me.

CHAPTER FOURTEEN

We think caged birds sing, when indeed they cry.
~John Webster

THE VOICES BREAK into the black abyss of unconsciousness first, the cold cloth on my forehead second. Athena and Vale are talking above me, which means I'm on the ground. My head and most of my upper body are cradled on something firm and warm, probably a lap. That's the one nice result of this problem. I can't believe that I straight up fainted. I'm not sure whether to be embarrassed or relieved. Hell, maybe I should thank him for keeping me from faceplanting on the floor or perhaps I should kick him in the balls for saying he has to fuck me to fix himself.

Don't get me wrong, part of me is completely digging that bit of it. The idea of him touching me on my neglected lady-parts makes those very same spots pay close attention to how close he is to me right now, but I'm not the Vale meat processor.

"She's awake and thinking something asinine if that goofy smile on her face is any indication," Athena says dryly.

"Hey, back off bird. I'll pluck you and make a hemorrhoid pillow out of your feathers," I grumble opening one eye to glare at her. I'm not ready to get up yet, my back and head are on Vale's lap, and it's a comfortable place that I'm not quite ready to vacate. It feels real and stable in a totally fucked up moment.

For a few minutes I can pretend that this is an entirely normal situation; I fainted, and a great looking man is treating me kindly. Yeah, that works out well. My eyes pop open and are immediately captured by Vale's. He smiles and I'm not sure whether I should run or hand him my bra in defeat.

When his eyes lighten even more and dance with that intensity that makes my skin feel too tight, the bra decision is a close one.

"I've had many reactions to the option of sex with me before, but never has someone fainted. I'm flattered," he teases.

"And arrogant," I add.

"That's a given, beautiful."

Frowning, I impulsively say, "Why do you call me beautiful? Is that like you saying, sweetie or honey?"

The smile remains, but it turns a bit more serious. "You are the first woman I've ever called beautiful." Looking at the slight frown between his eyes, I'm trying to decide who's more surprised him or me?

"Why do you say it?"

His finger traces the bridge of my nose then moves down to trace my bottom lip and in a move too fast for me to follow, I'm lifted to my feet and find myself standing face to face with him. He takes a step forward, and I take one backward and then he's walking me back until I bump against the cold, stone wall.

He doesn't stop there. Oh no, he keeps going until he's flush against me. Resting his forehead against mine, he leans to the side enough to slide his hand along the outside of my leg and to lift it at the knee to wrap it around his hip. He repeats this with the other one, and I find myself pinned against the wall with a warm, hard man between my legs. He's completely supporting me with his hands on my ass. Yes, my ass.

I like it.

"When I saw you the first time, it was like seeing the sun peeking into the utter darkness of this place. Drawn to it, I crawled out of the hole of pity I'd dug myself and basked in the warmth of that light. Then you smiled," he kisses my chin, then my cheek. "You smiled, and something inside of me awoke; in that moment I knew what it was to feel truly alive." He kisses the tip of my nose and then the other cheek. "When I tasted you, my soul unfurled and touched yours, full of want and greed and lust that burns so hot between us it eclipses the stars."

Breathlessly I say, "Those are some pretty words, hotstuff." Ugh, I sound like I ran up five flights of stairs, after eating an entire cake. Wait, did I seriously call him hotstuff?

Graceful, Mel. Epically so, you'll talk his shirt right off with that sexy phrasing.

"I will not be denied, Mel. I will *never* be denied when it comes to you. I will fuck you until I feel completely whole, I will lose myself in your body as many times as it takes to tie us together so irrevocably that for a time, we lose ourselves in each other. We will be one and anything that stands in my way will be torn through with prejudice I have not shown since creation," he says with such calm that if I hadn't been looking into the fervent emotion glowing in his eyes, I'd have thought him a liar.

When I take a breath, it hitches and before I can take another his hot mouth on mine takes away any words that I would've managed to sputter out. Letting the emotion take me in the heat of the moment, I grab the back of his head and meet him with as much passion as he's giving me. Only stopping when I know that continuing will end up with us doing something that will start a chain reaction that I'm not strong enough to deal with, not yet. There's too much I don't know.

Pushing at him I pull away to breathe air not saturated with the taste of him. He releases my ass and lets me slowly slide down his body to stand on my wobbling legs. He doesn't step away, but he takes his hands from me, giving me that space I need so desperately to get my brain working again.

Staring into his flushed face and glowing eyes I feel this absolute sense of destiny closing its tentacles around me in a tight fist, so tight that there's no escape for me—no matter how hard I try to fight it. Somehow this man plays a massive part in it. And for a solid ten seconds, I fucking hate it. No one wants to be told that they have to do something. We're all forever rebellious children.

"Tell me everything or you get nothing from me. There'll be no more secrets or any of that alpha male bullshit where you omit things to 'protect' me. It's straight up, or not at all. There are no exceptions to this." I try to cross my arms and look serious, but his mouth is still slightly parted, and I can see the sheen of moisture on his bottom lip from our kiss. Which makes me pose in such a way that I look like I'm awkwardly holding my boobs up with my forearms.

The knowledge that I affected him in such a way gives me cool tingles on my skin. I did this to him. Me. In my ugly uniform and my sloppy hair. My complete lack of makeup and the only splash of color on my face being the Eye-of-Odd and the dark circles under my eyes. As I bask in that fact, I go over what he said in my scattered brain. The feminist in me wants to demand he release me and stomp off in a huff, the horny woman in me though—she loves it and the thought of someone wanting me that much—gives me more power than anything else in my mind.

Damnit.

Carefully, and rather clumsily, I extract myself from in between him and the wall. I manage to not run to the podium holding the book, but it's a near thing. I'm pretty sure I jogged a little, it was fast enough that there's a smirk on his handsome face.

"As you wish." It takes me a few seconds to realize what he did.

"Did you make a Princess Bride reference?"

"I've been here ten years, not a hundred, Mel."

"Now, get to talking." I slip the amulet over my head without thinking about it. Tucking it in my shirt, I feel it warm against my skin. This is mine, I know it is, and even if it weren't—I can blame the bird.

"Not that I want to interrupt this *thrilling* romantic dance you two are doing... but she does need to know," Athena says from her perch atop the cage.

Leaning my elbow next to the book I distractedly look through it while waiting for him to talk. He agreed and if I've learned nothing else about him—besides the fact that he kisses like a god—it'd be that he always does what he says.

"As you've gathered there are multiple dimensions or realms as some call them." I nod, and he continues, "I'm from this realm."

"Earth?" I ask.

"No, this realm that you're standing in." He points at the floor.

"Yeah, Earth." I look up at him, and he's looking at me like I did something wrong. "What?"

"Holy shit, you think you're still on Earth?" he demands. "Do you also think you're from that dirty realm?"

Gah, a lot of hate there for my home. "I was born there, Vale, that's why."

"The Path Keeper would have only been born *here*," he points again at the floor, "in the Path. I'm not sure what you've been told, but someone's lied to you." This gets my full attention. "There are only two creatures ever born in the Path. Its Keeper, and the Nothing King. I'm looking at the Keeper, and I am the Nothing. So, tell me what your father—the former Path Keeper—told you about him leaving us to become trapped in this shit hole?" The intensity is back on his face but not the good kind from before.

Wait, my father? "I don't understand. I know nothing about my sperm donor. Mom says that he was a war hero who died overseas." Vale, being Vale shakes his head and ruins every carefully crafted fantasy about my missing parent.

His voice gentles as he says, "Your father Gabriel was the former Path Keeper. He was supposed to guard this place and keep this," he waves his hand around the room, "Safe from what shit has befallen it. But when the worthless bastards that imprison us here came, he didn't return from one of his trips away." The angry light in his eyes dims, and he continues, "This was once a haven for World-Walkers like us—a place to come and safely rest or even live. Once upon a time, I could protect them from those that use World-Walkers for their abilities. A Path Keeper is the only one who can keep the Path open, uncorrupted. Gabriel knew this and still chose his own life over all the ones here."

He pauses and studies my face then when he makes his decision, finishes with, "Do you know anything about him at all?"

I swallow the misplaced hurt that those words cause, as the glass world that I never believed in but wanted to, crumbles around me. "No," I croak out, unsure of what else to say about the man I never met. That left my poor mother to fend for a child alone, in a time when it was much more difficult for a single mother to exist. She did it, I had a good childhood, albeit an alternative one, but still good.

Giving it to me broke her.

"So, what," I clear my throat of the tears that are burning in the back of it, "what do I do to make things right?"

"You accepted things rather easily and quickly, Mel. Are you sure you don't think you're in a delusion?" Athena asks, hopping back down onto the podium. I mull over the answer in my head. Do I?

Am I truly ready to accept that this is all fact? That there are magical creatures all around me, hundreds of other worlds, that my father was a coward? Other than the initial doubt and the occasional feeling of surrealistic shit, I've been pretty accepting.

I called my therapist and questioned her for a solid hour —that I paid two-hundred dollars for—I've ruled out everything else, my therapist told me. Although, I left out the seeing thing's parts, that I have absolutely no symptoms of a psychotic break or a schizophrenic episode. At least, other than the seeing shit.

No mania, no ideas of grandeur, no violence.

"I've ruled out everything else, which leaves the only option being that this is reality. If it's not? Well, I guess I've had a blast?" Athena laughs and brushes her head against my hand.

I turn back to Vale. I'll deal with all this news about my...

father, later. Right now, I need to deal with the more important task at hand. How do I save all these people?

"What's the first thing we need to do?" I ask, drawing on inner strength to ignore the stupid hot tears that managed to leak out.

"Start taking the Path back, a piece at a time," Vale says softly, wiping his thumb under each of my eyes.

"Then what?"

His smile is all teeth and absolute satisfaction as he says, "We kill the intruders."

"With what? Bedpans and sheets?" I can't help but ask.

There isn't exactly an arsenal of guns laying around anywhere. And from what I've seen the guards have swords and these cattle prod looking things that can take any of the inhabitants down in one or two zaps. With the exception of Vale and Tav—wait, Vale version 2.0.

"Do not discount the lethality of anyone trapped in this place, Mel. Including you."

This makes me laugh. Yeah, sure I can bend a few fingers and probably break a kneecap or two, but there is nothing in my incredibly limited set of skills that I can call lethal.

"See, that's the human part of you thinking." He wiggles his fingers me. "You are the one this place breathes for. Make it remember. I'm sure the uncontrolled parts have called out for you."

I think back to the walls breathing and wonder if maybe he's right. It's too much of a coincidence to ignore. He did say the place breathes for me. I'm not the shiniest apple on the tree, but I do have moments of clarity, and this is one of them.

"First, we teach you to talk to the Path, and then we start strengthening up the prisoners here."

"What happens once we do?" I ask.

Leaning down he softly kisses me but pulls away before it can deepen into anything more than a brief meeting of lips.

"I get to bury my teeth in your skin."

Well, I called that, didn't I?

Next book in the Unsylum Series:

As the Crow Flies - Book Two

ACKNOWLEDGMENTS

I want to thank everyone who had a hand in getting this bad boy out there. My Admin team, Brandy Reece, Neva Perkins (sorry you died in this one), Natasha Nicholson. Without those three ladies I'd never get anything done.

I want to thank my street team for getting everything out into the world for you. You ladies make a huge difference in book-land for me, thank you!

Lumpytots, yes babe, you. Thank you for always standing by me. You make me calm, you make me food, you make me happy.

Thank you, my dear offspring. I love you all.

Most of all, thank you—whoever you are, for reading this mess.

ABOUT THE AUTHOR

Zoe is the type of person that thinks writing about herself in the third person is giggle worthy. She also laughs at those T-REX costumes that flap about when you run. Zoe has a hard time writing about normal things and has a soft spot for the antihero and the monster in the closet. For all we know they're lonely and trying to make friends. They're just doing it badly.

Www.zoeparkerbooks.com
https://www.facebook.com/ZoeParkerAuthor
https://www.facebook.com/groups/ZoesSavagesquad

ALSO BY ZOE PARKER

Facets of Feyrie Series - Urban Fantasy

Elusion, Book One

Ascension, Book Two

Deception, Book Three

Obliteration, Book Four

A (RH), multiple-mayhem series, The Fate Caller Series:

Cadence of Ciar, Book One

Rhythm of Rime, Book Two

Timing of Trick, Book Three

Ballad of Bael, Book Four

Unsylum Series

Up with the Crows - Book One

As the Crow Flies - Book Two

Stone the Crows - Book Three

Made in the USA
Monee, IL
03 February 2021